Alice

AND THE GRUMP

L. MOONE

ISBN-13: 9781913930912

CONTENTS

CONTENTS

CHAPTER ONE

*** Alice ***

It's bright and early when I head down to my little coffee shop right on Teddington High Street. Although the morning is still young when I open the shutter and unlock the front entrance, I can already tell it's going to be unseasonably warm for September.

It's just going to be me for a while, in my quiet little corner in West London. Until Amber and Richard come in to start working on his next novel, that is. Ever since Amber moved out of my flat once the two of them became an item, they've been taking their own sweet time getting ready in the morning. Not like before, when she'd walk down with me, and he'd show up minutes after opening.

I can't blame them. They're in love. They're happy.

I wish I had that. Over the span of this calendar year, every single one of my friends has found love, and as a result, pulled away. Amber is the only one I even see anymore on the regular, whereas we all used to meet every single Saturday before. How on earth am I the last one left waiting on the sidelines while cheering everyone on? Oh, the irony…

But I do enjoy having a moment to myself every morning while setting things up for the day to come. I inhale deeply and enjoy the familiar aroma of coffee beans and cinnamon that permanently seems to cling to the place. My own little refuge from the real world. Well, for all intents and purposes, it's mine. I might technically just work here, but as the coffee shop's one and only permanent employee, I still get to be my own boss.

I take a moment to appreciate the little haven I've created here. The boss has always been hands-off and absent. He just pays the bills, including my salary, and leaves the rest of the day-to-day affairs to me. As a result, everything you see—from the decor to the menu—has been my doing. *Coffee to the Rescue,* indeed, I tell myself while switching on the espresso machine and preparing the day's first brew.

I'm just lifting the cup to my lips, while scanning the quirky yet cozy interior of the cafe for any outstanding jobs that need doing this morning, when the door chime sounds behind me.

"You guys are up early today!" I turn around with a wide smile on my face, only to pause when I spot a stranger at the door. Tall and husky, with salt & pepper hair, and handsome enough to have just walked off the set of a TV show. He looks strangely familiar, even if I can't place him just yet.

"Sorry?" he asks.

"Oh, excuse me, I thought—Never mind. What can I get you on this fine Monday morning?"

He looks up at me with one raised eyebrow, clearly not in the mood for small talk. "Cappuccino," he replies in a gruff voice.

I suppress a smile. Okay then, Mr. Grumpy Pants. "Well, you've come to the right place for that." I do take my coffee very seriously, though maybe not as seriously as he seems to take himself.

He grunts in response, but I refuse to let his moodiness get to me. I recognize the type. He's probably just not a morning person. Or he's got some important meeting lined up at work, which he's stressing about. In any case, I'm not taking it personally.

"Takeaway or having it here?" I ask.

"Takeaway."

I don't bother to ask for the size or if he wants any flavors or add-ons. He doesn't seem the type to appreciate more questions. As I make his drink, I catch myself stealing glances at him while he's inspecting the cafe's interior. What's his story? He's in his forties, maybe even nearing fifty. And he has an air about him that suggests he's used to being in charge. He's solid and built for strength as well as comfort, the way he fills out that white button down shirt with the sleeves rolled up halfway up those thick forearms… Here's a guy who could absolutely dominate me without breaking a sweat. *Swoon.* The only thing gentle about him is the pale green of his eyes and the fullness of his lips.

Who the hell is he? I've seen this face somewhere and I'm pretty sure it wasn't here. I never forget a customer.

When I hand him his coffee, he pays for it without saying a word. But before he walks out the door, he turns to me and says, "I'm sorry, I'm not much of a morning person."

"Well, that's why it's called Coffee to the Rescue."

"Sorry, what?"

"The name of the shop. Coffee to the Rescue." I point at the cursive lettering on the wall behind me. He really doesn't have a sense of humor, which tickles me even more for some reason. Still, I do my best to suppress the wide grin that's itching to appear on my face.

"Ah." He pauses for a moment, then surprises me with the briefest of smiles, revealing a row of perfectly white teeth to match the rest of his well polished appearance. And that's enough to nearly knock the wind out of me.

"That's clever."

"Thanks," I mumble, still rattled by how much his smile affected me.

He nods and raises his cup at me before walking

out the door. I think I spot a twinkle in his eye as he does so, which gets my heart racing some more. Well, that was weird. And where have I seen this hunky wardrobe of a man before? I finally take a sip of my now lukewarm coffee to calm my nerves.

That's when the door chimes again, and Amber and Richard appear.

"Alice, was that who I thought it was, leaving the shop just now?" Amber asks me, wide-eyed and out of breath.

"Huh?"

Richard smiles warmly at me. "Good morning, Alice."

"Morning," I mumble. "I'm sorry, was that *who?*"

"Jack Cleary, the famous chef?!" Amber urges. "You know, from that cooking competition. The one who tends to make the contestants cry when they screw up?"

I turn to look out the glass front of the shop, but he's long gone by now. Jack-effing-Cleary. *Holy crap*. That's why I thought I'd seen him before! I have, except it was on TV!

"You know what? I think it might have been, yes," I say, while coolly taking a sip from my cup.

"That's crazy! Isn't that just crazy? The people you meet in a coffee shop, eh?" Amber gently bumps her elbow into Richard, who smiles at her before putting his arm around her shoulder.

"You meet the best people in coffee shops," he says.

They're so cute together, I kind of hate it. Because it's exactly what I want for myself. But I always end up being the cheerleader of everyone else's relationship, instead of finding one for myself… Bleh, jealousy is such a dirty emotion. I take a deep breath and close my eyes, picturing Jack Cleary's face when he finally smiled at me. Jesus, that was something else, wasn't it? I don't think I've ever seen him smile on TV. He's always so strict, almost scary. I guess that isn't just a persona; he's quite the grump, even in real life. Except for that one little crack in his veneer. And the way he looked at me when he was leaving. As if there are hidden depths to be discovered in him.

I must be losing my damn mind.

Amber and Richard take a seat at their regular tables and start unpacking their laptops. I make their regular drinks almost on autopilot. Once I'm done with that, the delivery from the local bakery arrives. And then, the mail.

I'm about done stocking up the display case, when an envelope with old-fashioned cursive handwriting catches my eye. It's mixed in with the regular bills and things, but addressed to me personally, which is unusual. Most mail that arrives tends to be in the name of the coffee shop, or the illustrious owner of this place. Curiosity gets the better of me and I open it immediately.

As soon as I start reading, my heart sinks.

* Jack *

It's perfect, just as I knew it would be. The location on the High Street, the London suburb of Teddington itself… Once I knock through the dividing wall and combine both the shops back into one, it's going to be just the right size, while still leaving plenty of room for a substantial kitchen and storage area in the back. My plans to branch out into casual eateries are finally taking shape.

The only problem—Well, it's not really a problem. The landlord promised to get the coffee shop as well as the art gallery next door vacated, and then I'll be able to get possession shortly after. The three months of notice period will allow me time to finalize my plans with my architect.

But, if it's all so perfect, then why do I feel like there's disaster looming around the corner? Since leaving Coffee to the Rescue, which admittedly is a rather fitting name for the place, I'm finding it difficult to stay on track. As it is, optimism isn't one of my strong suits, but this exact level of dread is a new low, even for me.

That girl, Alice—as per her name tag—clearly has no idea what's about to happen, or she wouldn't have been anywhere near as cheerful. I do feel for her. It's not easy having to relocate an established business. A lot of work and expense, neither of which she would have budgeted for.

But, such is life. And this isn't personal. I've been looking for a suitable location in this area—close enough to my home in Kingston, yet far enough from my flagship fine dining restaurant to not cannibalize its business—and the young man who owns the building is looking to raise the rents in line with market rates. It's completely above board. Just business as usual.

If I wasn't interested in renting the place, someone else surely would. It's in a prime location in a sought-after area. If the cafe is profitable enough, she should easily be able to move just around the corner and keep most of her regular clientèle at a cheaper rate than what she must be paying right now. And if not, then she probably wouldn't stay in business in the long term anyway…

Still… All the justifications in the world can't make me shake this feeling. I'm not even sure what it is exactly. Unease. Restlessness. Guilt?

This is why I don't socialize much, outside of a very small circle of associates. Why I like to keep myself focused on business only. A kitchen, I know how to handle. It's easy, with clear systems in place. People, and the emotional entanglements they inspire, are much harder to navigate. I'm not cut out for that sort of thing.

I put on some dark sunglasses as I turn the corner away from the High Street and head towards a nearby green area. It's become a habit to try and maintain some privacy, something that I've become accustomed to doing whenever I'm out and about. But unlike Central London, or even my hometown of Kingston upon Thames, Teddington is so quiet at this time of day, I hardly pass anyone on my way who could possibly recognize me.

It's nice, mostly because I know the solitude I'm observing right now is deceptive. Come evening, when everyone is back from work, this High Street will be a bustling hub of activity. I already counted a number of well established bars, pubs, and restaurants along my way. All of them must be doing good business, or they wouldn't have survived this long.

And on the weekends, this area with its parks and greenery will attract young families from surrounding areas as well. There will be plenty of footfall. My other restaurants around the city are formal and strictly reservation-only, but here I plan to do something new. Something more accessible. Once word gets out, I'll certainly get bookings too, but I finally want to be able to cater to walk-ins as well… I want to bring quality food to the masses, rather than only the affluent few.

I make my way through the gates of Bushy Park

and take a deep breath of fresh morning air. It's still pleasantly cool, even though the weather forecast predicted it's going to be quite warm for late summer. It'll be nice to come here more often, whenever I drive down to oversee the construction work at the new location.

Maybe I'll see that girl, Alice, again whenever I'm here. Then I'll be able to figure out if she and her quirky coffee shop have landed on their feet. Because that cappuccino was so good, it'd be a tragedy if she had to close her doors forever.

CHAPTER TWO

*** Alice ***

It takes me multiple tries to be able to understand what I'm reading. The letter, which is printed on some fancy-sounding law firm's letterhead, is professional and to the point, but my brain is having trouble processing it.

"You guys?" I call out and surprise myself with how shrill my voice sounds.

"Alice, what's wrong?" Amber asks, rushing over.

Richard also gets up and joins us at the counter.

"This just came… Am I reading it correctly?" I hand the letter over to Amber and Richard, who start to study it together. "My boss has suddenly passed away and his heir wants to close the coffee shop?"

"Well that's not good," Richard remarks under his breath.

"Right," I mumble.

"You're joking!" Amber complains.

I watch as the two of them read in silence.

"I guess you were right, huh?" I remark, finally.

"About?" Amber looks up.

"Didn't you question whether this place was profitable only a couple of months back?" I ask. "And I told you I wasn't worried, because my boss owns the building—well, I mean, *owned* the building, apparently; poor guy. I should have listened to you. I guess the figures must look really bad, or I wouldn't be getting shut down now."

"We started working on the marketing right away though, didn't we? Your profits should be up considerably since April," Amber tells me.

All the work she's done for me, promoting this place on social media and such, it did bear fruit. Business *is* up. But I have no concept of how much money I *should* be earning. I don't even know what the usual rents are like around here.

I'm not an entrepreneur; I'm just someone who fell into this job randomly and stuck around because I liked playing coffee shop owner. So far, I've had all the decision making power and none of the risks. My regular paycheck, plus the occasional tips, meant that profits, losses, and the bottom line were never anything I had to worry about personally.

I'm going to have to get a new job. Somewhere other than *here*, which has become my home of sorts… Ugh, I'm really going to miss this place! It's become a part of me, my identity. If I'm not Alice from the coffee shop, then who even am I?

"You could draw up a business plan and apply for

a loan, and then find a new location nearby," Richard suggests.

"I can do that?" I ask.

"You could get some private investors as well," Amber chimes in.

"As if I know people with money like that!" I argue.

Amber turns her head to stare at Richard with her eyebrows raised in expectation. "Maybe *we* do?"

Richard looks lost in thought, with his brow furrowed and lips pursed slightly. "The bank is a good first option. Angel investors are more likely to bet on a business that already has some formal funding. I can help you draw something up."

"Would you?" My heart is still racing and my palms are sweating. "I don't want to be a bother, but I know exactly nothing about writing a business plan."

"Don't worry about it," Richard tells me, his face softening into a smile. "It's the least I can do."

"And I'll help with the marketing part," Amber adds.

I press my lips together and look at her, then at him, then back at her. Tears are prickling in my eyes and my palms have grown cold and clammy. "Thank you so much! This means a lot to me." I try to wipe my hands on my apron, but it doesn't help.

"Aw, don't be ridiculous," Amber says. "Of course

we'll help you. In fact, I should get a FundMe campaign going for the coffee shop. Just to give you some starting capital to show to the bank."

"How much time do we have?" Richard asks, scanning the letter again.

"It says I have three months."

He mutters something under his breath, but I can't quite understand him. My head feels light and my knees are weak, so I steady myself against the counter and take a few deep breaths. What a fucking morning.

"You guys, I don't know what I'd do without you," I breathe.

"Relax. We'll figure something out," Amber tells me, rubbing my shoulder.

Richard smiles briefly and nods at me.

"Remember not too long ago, when I was going through a crisis of my own?" Amber asks. "You were telling me something about being open to new opportunities."

I frown. That does sound like something I'd say, but I'm not quite seeing the relevance.

"It worked out great for me." She nods at Richard to make her point. "So, why shouldn't it turn out well for you too?"

I open my mouth to say something, but can't think of anything, so I just keep staring at her. *Who are you and what have you done to the real Amber?*

"We'll do our best to help you figure this out,"

Richard agrees.

If he says so. I focus on steadying my breath, then force myself back into action. A few remaining pastries still have to be loaded into the display case, the counter wiped down, the espresso machine emptied out. So much to do, so little time. To think that only a short while ago my biggest concern was my lack of a love life. And already the universe has thrown a challenge at me that is so big, I won't have time to even think about dating.

* Jack *

A long walk to try and clear my head, and several phone calls to my architect and my PA later, and it's almost noon. I'm still finding myself roaming around Teddington.

Just checking out the local area, I tell myself. That's not really it, though it's a charming part of Greater London.

Sure, I am observing the shops on the High Street open up, watching the cars go by, and the mothers pushing their prams across the pavement on the way to the supermarket. And I'm wondering if I could get permission for some outdoor seating in the summers. There certainly is enough room for it.

But I'm not really as focused on these things as I would like to be. And most of them don't really matter, anyway. Any restaurant of mine is going to attract attention, no matter what. Such are the perks of getting to be on TV fairly regularly.

That same odd sense of heaviness that has followed me around all morning still lingers. And it's distracting me.

I could kill for a good cup of coffee… And the one that I had this morning was exquisite. I should find out what machine she's using. And what beans. I would put money on the fact that both were imported from Italy.

With renewed purpose in my step, and a fresh list of justifying excuses in my head, I make my way back to the same location. Coffee to the Rescue. It's certainly going to rescue me from this brain fog.

And maybe if I talk to the girl, Alice, a little bit, I might assuage these inconvenient feelings I've been having as well.

Even the door chime sounds oddly comforting when I enter. I hadn't noticed how it had a slightly different tune from almost every other shop I've been to: warmer, somehow. More welcoming.

This time, a few of the tables inside the cafe are occupied. Alice is in the process of serving one of her customers towards the rear of the shop, before turning around, tray in hand, to greet me.

"Welcome back!" she says, a wide smile appearing on her face.

I clear my throat and mumble a greeting.

"Cappuccino, takeaway? Or something else this time?" she asks.

She remembers my order, which is good. But then again, it was hardly a complicated choice.

"Yes to the cappuccino, but maybe I'll have it here…" I scan the display case beside the cash counter. These sandwiches and baked goods weren't here yet this morning. That means they're fresh. Perfect.

"And a cinnamon roll. Thanks."

She smiles and rings up my order, then she picks up the cinnamon roll with a pair of tongs and places it on a pink and white polka dot porcelain plate, before wiping a singular crumb away that ends up on the counter. Good attention to detail. I approve.

It's hard to not look at these things with a critical eye when you're in the food industry yourself.

She turns around and starts making my coffee. I observe a slight tremble in her hand when she picks up the cup and places it underneath the nozzle of the coffee maker. Am I making her nervous?

I mean, I do tend to have that effect on people. I should be used to it, but right now, it's making me uneasy all over again. There's that guilt again, tripping me up.

She's probably just weirded out, because I'm not chatty like most of her other customers would be. Silence tends to make normal people uncomfortable.

"Lovely day we're having," I remark.

"Yes. Yes, it is." She looks back and smiles briefly, then carries on frothing the milk, before expertly pouring it into my cup, leaving perfect swirl marks on top.

"Here you go…" She looks me in the eye for a moment, and my heart nearly stops. There's something off in her gaze now. Something I didn't notice this morning. "…Mr. Cleary."

I exhale, suddenly realizing that I'd been holding my breath. She recognized me; that's all.

"Ah, you can just call me Jack," I tell her.

She smiles and looks away again. "I'm Alice. Sorry, we don't get a lot of famous people in here."

I make a face and shake my head. "Ah, that's all just… Forget it." It's all bullshit. That's what I want to tell her. That I'm just a guy with a passion for food, but the fame part of it is just fluff, a sometimes inconvenient side effect. But I've learned over the years that people don't tend to like it when you say things like that. Apparently, it comes across as arrogant.

"But I'm glad you liked the coffee enough to come back," she adds, smiling again.

There's a tickle in my chest, which makes me smile back at her, before I take out my wallet and place a £20 note on the counter. "Keep the change."

"Thanks," she says as she counts out my change

and puts half of it in the charity collection box next to the cash register, and the other half into the tip jar.

"You make a lovely cup of coffee, as I'm sure all these people here will agree," I tell her. It feels funny to compliment her. Awkward. Even if it's deserved. I'm much more used to offering people constructive criticism than praise.

Her eyes widen, and go slightly moist all at the same time. She's full-on staring at me now. I guess I'm staring back. I'm not sure I like how off-balance that makes me feel. How is she having this effect on me?

"Thanks. The cinnamon rolls aren't half bad either," she says. "Even if I didn't bake those myself."

I suppress a smile and nod. "Cheers."

As I take a seat somewhere out of the way, the door chime goes off, signaling the arrival of more customers, no doubt. I'm glad to see that footfall is picking up now. Hopefully Alice will be able to retain most of her regulars if she finds another location nearby. And maybe those same people wouldn't mind grabbing a sensibly priced gourmet burger at my new restaurant once it opens up.

"Did you know about this?" A loud female voice—not Alice—attracts my attention.

I can't help but observe the interaction at the counter. An elegantly dressed brunette in her early thirties stands in front of Alice, holding a letter in her hand while gesturing irately.

Oh boy.

"Clara, hi… Yes, I got one just like it this morning," Alice tells her. Her voice is more hushed, but still loud enough for me to hear every word if I concentrate.

I take a sip of coffee and pretend not to eavesdrop.

"How on earth am I supposed to just pack up and move an entire art gallery within three months? I have events lined up months in advance! And rather than focus on that, I'm going to have to scout for a new location now? This is a disgrace! And that too, coming up to the holiday season," the woman, Clara, complains.

"Tell me about it. I'm about to be out of a job," Alice agrees. "In fact I've been waiting for Deedee to come in and cover for me so I could have a chat with you about what you're planning to do next."

Clara throws her hands up in the air in frustration. "I don't know. This has taken me completely by surprise."

"Same."

"Too bad about Mr. Sinclair, huh? He's always been good to us."

Clara scoffs. "Yeah. Too bad his son prefers money over loyalty."

Alice smiles a sad smile. "Maybe. Who knows

what the whole story is, though. Have you ever met the son? Would it be worth reaching out, you think?"

"I doubt it. If he was open to negotiations, he would have started a dialogue himself. Rather than send his lawyers after us to evict us without so much as a warning."

"True, true…" Alice shrugs. "Cup of Earl Grey? On the house?"

Clara sighs deeply, then nods. "Why not. Thanks, Alice."

"You're welcome."

For a brief moment, Alice looks up in my direction. I quickly pretend to be fully focused on my cup of coffee instead.

So, she knows. And it seems she's the manager here, rather than the actual owner of the shop. That makes more sense, considering she must be in her late twenties at the most.

I wonder if she'd like a job as a hostess; at least that's something I can help her with… I still feel bad for the other woman—the owner of the art gallery next door. Transitions are always hard, but if her business is viable, she will land on her feet eventually.

Not my responsibility, I tell myself. Even if I wasn't interested in renting this building, someone else surely would. Still, I can't shake the feeling that I should be doing something more to help.

CHAPTER THREE

*** Alice ***

It's still early when I settle down at a two-seater table in the otherwise empty coffee shop, my thoughts consumed by the task at hand. This place has been my home—a fantasy of sorts—even if it was never truly my own. But Richard and Amber's suggestions yesterday got me thinking that maybe it could be. It's going to take more than hopes and dreams to make it a reality, though. Which is why I came in extra early today to start working on a plan.

Repeated Google searches on how to create a business plan only confused me more. I'm more of an intuitive thinker rather than a planner. But no bank is going to give me a loan based on a mere *feeling* that I can make this thing work. I'm guessing the bank manager isn't going to be swayed by a bribe of lifetime free takeaway coffee and cinnamon rolls either…

As I ponder my next move, Richard and Amber enter the shop. They both wave to me and come over to sit down.

"Hey, Alice," Richard says. "How are you doing?"

"I'm okay, considering," I reply. "Thanks for coming in so early."

"No problem," Amber chimes in, "we're happy to help in any way we can."

Richard pulls out a notebook and starts walking me through the necessary components of a business plan. He explains everything from the financial projections to formal business structures. It's a lot to take in, but I feel much more confident with his guidance and furiously try to keep up by taking notes.

"Every good business plan also contains a robust marketing strategy, to demonstrate how you'll grow the business to be able to pay back the loan," Richard says.

"That's where I come in," Amber says. "On top of what we've already been doing with various influencers, I've got a whole bunch of new ideas as well."

"You guys…" I smile gratefully at both of them. "You're too kind."

"Don't mention it. I like coming here every day. The last thing I need is to lose my one and only writing spot," Richard says.

Amber nods her head. "And I'd be heartbroken if I didn't get to have your vanilla hazelnut macchiatos anymore."

"You know that other coffee shops serve those as

well, right? I didn't invent that drink," I remark.

"I know. It just doesn't taste the same anywhere else." Amber shrugs.

Her voice sounds so earnest, it makes me smile. People do seem to enjoy my coffee… Even a certain famous chef, who even turned up a second time yesterday while these two were out for lunch. That has to count for something.

Filled with fresh motivation and excitement, I'm ready to start working on everything Richard has explained so far. My earlier doubts and fears fade as we spend the next hour or so brainstorming and refining my plans together. By the time the first regular customers of the day start pouring in, I feel like I have a solid foundation to work with myself.

It's going to be a long road, but with Richard and Amber's help, I'm one step closer to pulling this thing off. Maybe Amber, quoting my own words to me yesterday, was spot on. This might turn out to be an amazing opportunity, rather than a disaster like I first thought.

* Jack *

My morning is hectic, as it usually is. Issues with suppliers, staffing problems, and calls to figure out the schedule for an upcoming TV appearance take up hours. Still, overshadowing all these day-to-day nuisances is that same lingering feeling of unease that's been following me ever since I visited that coffee shop in Teddington yesterday. Coffee to the Rescue. Guilt is a powerful motivator.

There's a knock on the door to my office, and Carrie appears with a tray of coffee and biscuits. Eleven o'clock already?

"Thanks," I mumble, while taking a whiff of the fresh brew before my first sip. It's good, obviously; I've picked out the coffee beans we use throughout my business myself. But somehow, it's missing something for me today.

I'd planned to figure out the secret behind Alice's excellent coffee yesterday when I swung by there the second time. But when I overheard the conversation between her and the woman from the art gallery, my ulterior motive was forgotten. In the end I rushed out of there as soon as I emptied my cup and finished my cinnamon roll, all while Alice was busy serving another customer.

"Remember, you have an appointment to sign the final paperwork for the lease at one," Carrie tells me.

I lean back, cup in hand. "Right. Could you remind me of the address?"

She nods, before rifling through some papers on my desk. "Here it is."

I glance over at the formal looking letterhead from the law firm representing the owner. They're in Twickenham, a short drive away which will lead me right through Teddington yet again.

I take another sip from my cup, then immediately put it back down. This coffee really isn't hitting the spot for me. I've still got a few things to do this morning, but maybe, once I'm done signing the papers… I could make a stop on the way back.

There's something about the place that has me coming back again and again.

Fact is, I'm intrigued. By the business, the quality of the coffee, or maybe… Maybe it's Alice herself. How she carries herself. Her manner in dealing with her customers. How she seems to manage the entire place all by herself as well as or even better than most business owners would, when in her own words she's just an employee.

It's her excellence, which has me obsessed. I see something in her which I've rarely seen in anyone else. The only two people who had something similar were chefs that worked under me, both of whom I mentored for a while. By now they've gone on to do amazing things on their own. Alice has the same potential.

I wondered yesterday if I ought to offer Alice a job, and now, I'm answering that question for myself with a resounding 'yes.' Anything, to see her succeed. And to keep her close. With that dilemma figured out, my next sip of coffee tastes a whole lot better already.

***

As I step inside, I feel strangely at home. The air is thick with the scent of Alice's signature roast, and the chatter of customers fills my ears. Alice is busy behind the counter, taking orders and making drinks with practiced ease. When she sees me, she flashes a bright smile my way.

I can't remember the last time anyone was this happy to see me. Usually, I have the opposite effect on people. It's nice. Something I could get used to. If I do end up hiring her, I might see a whole lot more of her radiant smile going forward. The prospect hits a nerve deep inside me.

I just want to help her, I tell myself. *Nothing more.*

"Hi, Jack! You're turning into a regular at this rate," she says, wiping her hands on a tea towel.

"I had some business in the area." I try to ignore the pang of guilt that hits me when I say that. "I figured I earned a cappuccino for my troubles. And another of those cinnamon rolls, if you can spare one."

Alice chuckles. It's a beautiful sound, which soothes my conflicted conscience and sparks a half-smile of my own.

"You're in luck, this is the last one."

I linger by the counter as Alice prepares my drink, her movements smoother than the last time I came in. I guess she was just rattled by the eviction letter. *Ah, there it is again. That sting of guilt, even deeper than before. Because that's all my fault.*

This was precisely the feeling I was trying to avoid by coming here and reaching out to her.

I find myself avoiding the sight I'd previously admired and stare aimlessly at the counter instead. Until I spot a large notepad with messy scribbles all over it. It stands out starkly against the otherwise neatly organized work surface.

"Working on something?" I remark, pointing at the notes.

Alice turns around, cup in hand, and makes a face. "Yeah… Sort of."

I meet her gaze for a second, but she instantly avoids it and looks at the notes again. "It's a business plan."

"Oh? For what?" My ignorance sounds exactly as feigned as it is.

She pauses, then takes a deep breath. "Since you're here, and you know… You're way more experienced than I am—" She's nervous. It's actually quite endearing, more so because it's unnecessary. I came here to help her and she's presenting me with the perfect opportunity herself.

It strikes me just how attractive she is. A radiant example of female beauty, soft and curvaceous in all the right places. No wonder I keep on wanting to come back to her. Good thing I swore off that sort of thing years ago when I realized I had nothing to offer on that front. And anyway, she's too young for me.

"Yes?" I ask with a hopefully disarming smile on my face.

"Would you…?"

I nod. "Of course. What is it?"

She scans our surroundings for a second. All the other customers are occupied in their own little conversations, creating a comforting hum inside the coffee shop. This lull in activity is the perfect chance for a chat. She quickly plates my cinnamon roll, processes my payment, and gathers her notes. I pick up my coffee and gesture her over to the same quiet table near the wall which I'd selected for myself yesterday.

She awkwardly slides a chair back for herself and pauses. "I'm so sorry to intrude on your well deserved coffee break, but…"

I make a dismissive gesture and smile again. As if I could refuse her anything. "It's no bother. Tell me about your business plan."

Alice takes a seat and stares at the notepad in her lap. "Okay, so the building is being vacated, and if I want to keep doing this, I'm going to need to apply for a small business loan."

I raise an eyebrow. She's looking to open her own café. So much for offering her a job, then. I try to fight the wave of disappointment that washes over me.

"Right. That's a pretty big step." Still, this is an excellent opportunity for me to be of use in a different capacity, isn't it? So what if she wouldn't be working for me? So what if I don't see her every day?

She smiles apologetically. "I know. But I figured, I've learned enough since I started here to make it work."

"Oh, I don't doubt it," I say. Especially if she can keep the quality up.

"So, here's what I've got so far. I'm only asking since you're in the industry yourself..." She puts the notepad on the table and slides it over to me.

On second thought, her notes aren't that messy at all. Her handwriting is neat and regular; she just has a lot of corrections and added thoughts scribbled into the margins which made it hard to read upside-down and across the counter.

I leaf through the pages, scanning over the headings of her business plan until I reach the end: the marketing plan is written in a distinctly different handwriting.

"This looks comprehensive," I say. Honestly, her plan is very impressive. I don't know why I can't just say that. People love to get compliments, don't they? I'm sure she would. Plus, she deserves it. "You did all of this yourself?"

She presses her lips together and shakes her head.

"I've had help. A *lot* of help."

I nod and start reading the first page in depth. "Whoever's been helping you clearly knows what they're doing."

"Yeah… He used to work in banking."

I glance up at her for a brief moment. She has a man helping her. Of course she does. A beautiful young woman like her, she's obviously not going to be single. I don't know why that almost disappoints me all over again. It's not like I'm interested in her that way! Absolutely not!

"Okay, so the main thing any loan officer at a bank will be looking for is whether you'll be able to repay the loan on time. You need to go heavy on the facts and figures; financial projections and such. Ideally, you'd have an accountant work on these with you."

"Okay, but how will we be able to make these projections? Aren't they just guesses?" she asks.

"Educated guesses, sure. Based on your observations here," I gesture at the other occupants still enjoying their hot beverages and baked goods, "how many customers do you get per day; what's the average order value; how many become recurring customers; what are your material costs and overheads, including rent and an initial budget for renovations; what's your profit margin… Figure those things out and you can make some fairly accurate predictions. Then, with the help of your planned marketing activities, you aim to increase footfall, which earns you more recurring business eventually."

"Right." She leans back with a thoughtful expression on her face.

"You'll speak to your existing vendors to make sure they'll follow you to the new business, unless you want to make changes to the menu. Maybe try to increase your margins where you can without upping the prices, at least at first. But honestly, what you've got here is brilliant in terms of quality. If you try to cut costs and sacrifice quality in the process, you might not be able to retain your existing customers and you should be prioritizing retention alongside new customer acquisition. And—something which I ignored when I was starting out—do account for a reasonable salary for yourself! And allow yourself space in the budget to hire help early on, because you're going to want to still have a life by the end of it all."

Alice chuckles. "Oh, I'm not too worried about that last part. I'm here all day every day already as it is. I'm quite used to it."

Our eyes meet and linger for a second. She might sound cheerful, but there's something she's leaving unsaid.

"Take it from someone who's been there," I urge. "You can only give so much of yourself to your business before you burn out. And before you know it, you find yourself married to the work."

She stares up at me, her eyebrows slightly raised. I clearly struck a nerve. She must be wondering about how long that banker guy of hers will stick around if she starts working around the clock. In a moment of weakness, I almost reach out and touch her, such is my need to comfort her. But that's not my place.

God, she looks so vulnerable right now, but I must resist. I was only trying to help and encourage, and I've achieved the opposite. Bloody typical, that.

"Okay, so how much would I need to budget for that, then?" Alice asks finally. "I just have one part-timer right now other than me…"

Relieved that I haven't put her off the conversation entirely, I try to give her as much practical information as possible, while staying away from the emotionally loaded topics. We manage to speak for about fifteen minutes before she gets up to look after some newly arrived customers.

Meanwhile, I finish my coffee and eat the last bite of my cinnamon roll. It tastes even better than yesterday. Funny how things go sometimes. I came in here to talk to her about job opportunities, to see if I could help her get her career back on track somehow. Instead, her plans to reopen the coffee shop on her own have provided me with the perfect opportunity to make a real, lasting impact. This, at least, is something I know intimately.

Consequently, those feelings of guilt that had been following me around are starting to dissipate. Instead they've been replaced with something else... A deeper fascination, peppered with regret. I'm still keen to help her as much as I can, but she already has a knight in shining armor that's not me. Shame.

Not that I was keen on taking on that role for her! I wouldn't dream of it. I made the exact choice I was warning her away from years ago. And I firmly chose my work. For me, it wasn't a mistake, but for her... She can do better. She can have it all.

With someone else.

Alice finishes serving her customers just as I approach the counter.

"So, you think I can pull this off?" Her tone is reluctant, almost a little fearful. Once again, I want nothing more than to make her feel better. That's not my place, though. I wouldn't dream of overstepping any boundaries with her.

I pause for a moment, then pull out my wallet. I came here to be useful, didn't I? This is purely professional.

"You've got the makings of something special here, truly. I'd love to help out. Feel free to reach out with any questions, or—" Encouragement? Or commiserations, for when the banker boyfriend decides he doesn't want to play second fiddle to a budding hospitality business anymore? I leave the last part unsaid. It's mean-spirited and unnecessary.

I hand my business card to her. Our fingers brush past each other for the briefest moment when she takes it from me. *Call me… for anything.*

Alice studies the card for a few seconds, giving me the chance to recover. What the hell is wrong with me? Our hands touched, so what? All I want to do is help her land on her feet, that's all!

"My personal email and phone number are on there," I explain. What I actually mean is, nobody has those details. Mostly, I prefer it if Carrie acts as a buffer between me and the rest of the world. That's what I pay her for. But that would sound pompous and arrogant again, so I keep my mouth shut.

"Wow, thanks so much!" Alice beams at me. "You're a lifesaver."

I swallow hard, because I wasn't ready to hear that word. Surely she's just being nice and doesn't mean anything by it, because I'm nothing of the sort. I'm the whole reason she's in this predicament.

Her smile brightens up the room and my heart. I can hardly take my eyes off her.

How I wish I could promise her that everything is going to work out perfectly. That her plan will come together and she will get that loan she's aiming for, that her business is going to be a raving success. But I can't, because this is a cruel and unforgiving industry. Statistics tell us that most food businesses fail within the first few years. Just getting a bank loan will be a huge challenge, because they know the stats even better than I do.

Still, I'm going to do what I can to help her. Maybe I'll swing by here a few mornings a week to check in? It's the least I can do after causing her all this trouble in the first place. And maybe it's also what I want, selfishly, just for me. Just to drink her excellent coffee and earn me another one of those exquisite smiles every so often.

A lifesaver, she said just now. If only she knew the truth.

"Alright, I best be off. Maybe see you around," I tell her.

She's still holding my card in her hand and staring at me in wonder when I give her a little nod and head out the door. Not a moment too soon, otherwise I might say or do something that would get me in *real* trouble. And I can't have that.

CHAPTER FOUR

*** Alice ***

I can't sleep. For hours now, I haven't been able to put Jack's most recent visit out of my mind.

Why should a world-renowned chef and bonafide famous person come into my little coffee shop three times within two days? And on top of that, why should he take out the time to look over my business plan? There is no logical reason for it.

And then, when our hands touched ever so briefly towards the end... He took my breath away. Again.

I Google him and find out that he's a local. And from there I end up caught in a rabbit hole of watching interview after interview of him. Apparently he grew up in Kingston, that's why he opened up his first restaurant there as well. That's less than half an hour away from here. If he does spend a lot of time in the local area, then how come I've never spotted him before? I've been managing the shop for nearly four years now, and I'm certain the day before yesterday was the first time I saw him anywhere other than on TV.

Maybe I'm trying to find patterns where there aren't any. Maybe this is all just a big fat happy coincidence.

Unless… He did give me his card. I tucked it into my wallet and later transferred it into the little jewelry box on my nightstand like a precious treasure, where it remains even now. When I take it out at three in the morning to admire it again, I catch a whiff of what must be very expensive cologne. His scent; it's intoxicating. I barely noticed it back at the shop, because the aroma of freshly ground coffee and cinnamon masked it at the time.

But now… Alone in bed, with only the memories of our interactions to keep me company, I can't help but attach a deeper meaning to everything that's been going on.

How he came in the first time: so serious, almost grumpy… Yet I managed to get a few words and even a smile out of him. And how he's seemingly thawed further with every consecutive visit. When we chatted today, he didn't even seem like the same sharp tongued cooking show judge who manages to make aspiring chefs quake in their boots on TV. He was charming. Kind. Patient. And when our hands touched ever so briefly, I thought I would faint.

This card he gave me, I will cherish it forever. It has his personal number on it, even! Yeah, I'll cherish it, but I won't use it. He surely has more important things to do all day than to field calls from a nervous wannabe coffee shop owner like myself. No matter how helpful he appeared to be today. Every successive interview I watch of him seems to suggest that he's not usually so warm and open. So, what's the real story?

I close my eyes and allow myself to dream for a minute while his scent still fills my lungs.

Amber found her prince charming in Richard right there at the shop, back in April. I'd like to think that my encouragement had something to do with them getting together, but still. And Lauren, who runs a boutique around the corner, met her beau over coffee several months earlier.

Could Jack's arrival at my shop be part of a larger plan? Is it finally my turn to get my very own happy ending right there at Coffee to the Rescue ?

Maybe that's what he was hinting at when he warned me not to end up 'married to the work.' That's a funny choice of words, isn't it? And the way he said it, too. There was something personal behind that statement. Something painful. Like a part of him was trying to reach out to a part of me, I just hadn't realized it at the time.

The more videos of him I watch on YouTube, the more torn I feel. I've met him three times now. And I barely recognize the man I'm seeing on my phone.

Sure, he looks the same; his mannerisms are the

same, his voice, choice of words. It's all him. But the image he projects in these videos, the authority and gravitas with which he speaks… Well, it's similar to our first meeting, in a way. But it's like night and day away from the conversation we shared only twelve hours ago. I saw a side to him which is absent from all this footage. What does *that* mean?

It means he likes you.

I close my eyes again and try to figure out how that possibility makes me feel. Terrified, excited and mellow all at once. Because I like him too.

This is crazy. I should really get to sleep! Plus, if he really did like me like that, then why not just ask me out? A man like him would have the confidence to approach whoever he wants. So clearly, I'm indulging in school girl fantasies about someone who doesn't feel the same. Why would he? I'm not all that!

But every time I close my eyes, I see Jack's face, with a crooked little smile, telling me he'll see me around. And when I turn over, and hug my pillow tightly against my chest, I see how he cracked a little, when he spoke about maintaining a life outside work. Again and again and again.

Every time I replay that moment, I think I see more of *him* in front of me. The real him, which he doesn't show to just anyone. It does something to me, makes my insides all mushy and soft. And it makes me think of the sort of advice I usually give others.

To be open to possibilities. To see the beauty in life.

That last part, I saw from the very start. He's a gorgeous man, despite or perhaps because of his dad bod physique. If there's an entry for the term 'silver fox' in the dictionary, there ought to be a picture of him underneath, with that utterly perfect full head of gray streaked hair and meticulously styled beard. And those sparkly green eyes and that dazzling smile, which he seems to reserve for special occasions only… Or maybe, just for special people? Oh how I wish that to be true. But then, I'm not special, am I? I'm just the same old Alice, who's about to lose a coffee shop that was never really hers.

* Jack *

Another day, another mountain of work awaits. I'm tempted to put it all off, and make a stop for a takeaway cappuccino from what is quickly becoming my new favorite coffee destination. But I don't. Because that would be suspicious and inappropriate.

Alice may think I'm stalking her. Or much worse, she'll figure out that I'm the reason behind all her troubles. I'm not sure I can face that reality just yet. Once I help her get settled—which I've vowed to do sometime between reading her business plan yesterday afternoon and waking up this morning— everything will become self-evident. But at least then I can look back on it with a positive attitude. I will become the catalyst for her success in her eyes, rather than a threat to her entire existence. *A lifesaver*, she called me. I still can't get that word out of my head, and every time I think of how she looked at me when she said it, I want to rise to the occasion more. I want to earn the label. Maybe then I'll feel worthy of her smile.

Right now, I'm far from deserving, though. Everything is uncertain. She's obviously scared. I could see it in her eyes yesterday when we spoke. I wish I could take all those worries away from her and fast forward to a moment in time when she and her business have already landed on her feet.

And the strangest thing is, I don't even know why I need her to see me that way. Not as a disruptor, but as a support or a helping hand. I don't even know the girl, for Christ's sake! Although I wish to with all my being…

When I think back to how discouraged she looked during parts of our conversation yesterday, my palms grow cold and my chest begins to tighten. How I ached to hold her in my arms and tell her it was all going to be okay.

But she has someone already. And I'm not one to intrude. Hell, I'm not one for romance in general; I've never had the time to focus on such things. My life has always evolved around my first love: my career. And that's worked out pretty well for me; I've been wildly successful and could wish for nothing.

What's changed? Nothing, actually. I ought to stick to my core values and treat this as I would any other food related venture.

I brush aside the pile of tasks Carrie curated for me this morning and instead take out a fresh sheet of paper. In hurried scribbles, I record all my thoughts for Alice's business idea as if it were one of my own.

It doesn't take long for me to fill the paper. And another. And a third.

Pros and cons. Potential challenges and risk analysis. Rough projections based on my own analysis of the area. Estimated overheads if she moves to a slightly less prestigious address within Teddington itself…

In many ways it's a rehash of everything I read in her business plan yesterday, which her banker guy helped her put together, as well as my own for the restaurant. Her plan was well done. I'm glad it was, because it means she has a real chance at success.

But banks are reluctant to give credit anymore. Especially to first time business owners, and more so for perceived hobby businesses like coffee shops and cupcake bakeries. And her plan lacks in-depth industry knowledge. However, if she had an insider with a proven track record to partner with, the situation would look quite different…

I've always been about fine dining, until now with

my new casual eatery concept. Coffee shops have never been on my radar… But why not? She's an excellent manager for the day-to-day running of the place; she's proven so in her current role. It's the big picture stuff she might need help with, as well as the finances…

I put my pen down and stare at my notes, which are admittedly much, much messier than her plan from yesterday. It doesn't just feel right, it looks good too, captured in black-and-white.

My first instinct was to offer her a job. Then, I offered to help with her plan, informally. But actually… I ought to offer her an investment along with a mentorship perhaps. Something proper, a formal contract, looked over and sanctioned by my lawyers just to make sure I'm not missing anything…

"Carrie?" I call out and wait, until her head pops around the door to my office a few seconds later.

"Yes, Jack?"

"How's the rest of my morning looking? Can we squeeze in a meeting with legal? And get my financial advisor on the phone, as well."

She frowns and glances at the papers in front of me. But she knows better than to comment or question me about what I'm up to. "I'll see what I can do."

"Thanks, Carrie."

* Alice *

I've never had to drag myself into work against my will. Not once in four years, right until this morning. Everything feels difficult and like a chore. From having a shower to getting dressed, right up to my morning stock-take at the store. My brain is fuzzy and uncooperative, and my body feels lethargic. Everything takes me three times as long.

It's the lack of sleep. And the stress of not knowing where I will be in three months' time. I'm missing the comfort of my bed, where I spent all morning, hidden under the covers, half-asleep and dreaming about all sorts of things that could never be.

But with my curtains drawn and eyes tightly shut, the seductive scent that continued to cling to Jack's business card had been giving me all sorts of ideas. Most of them are best left unspoken… Because no matter what my late night fantasies tried to convince me of, the man has said exactly nothing to suggest he's interested in me too. And why would he be? I'm just the barista at a coffee shop he happened to visit, whereas he's at the top of his game.

By the time Amber and Richard get in, I'm on my third cup of coffee already, which is unusual. Not only did the caffeine not wake me up properly, it made me jittery and anxious.

"Hey, there," Amber greets me with a smile.

She looks fresh and energetic. So unlike how I feel.

"Morning, Amber. Richard." I nod at both of them, and attempt a smile, before quickly turning around to make their usual drinks.

"Where's that notepad?" Amber asks behind me. "I'd wanted to look over the marketing plan again this morning."

I point at my shoulder bag which is sitting on the floor and resting against the side of the counter.

The coffee maker sighs and hisses, the soundtrack to my daily life over the last four years. But it doesn't comfort me. It actually sounds hostile this morning.

I try to shake off my dumb thoughts and arrange both drinks on a tray. When I turn around, tray in hand, I find Amber eyeing me with a suspicious look on her face.

"Whose handwriting is this?" she asks, pointing at a few scribbles on the blank page facing the start of my business plan notes.

I instantly feel my cheeks and ears heating up. "That, uhh…"

A knowing grin breaks through Amber's formerly confused expression. "Okay… details, please?"

I don't even know why I'm so flustered. Probably because I don't know what to make of any of it.

"Remember when you arrived the other day and you spotted a certain famous—"

"Jack Cleary," she interjects.

"He came in again yesterday afternoon. Since he

seemed to be in a chatty mood, I asked him a few questions."

"No way! You got Jack-fucking-Cleary to check your business plan!"

Richard joins Amber on the opposite side of the counter and wraps an arm around her shoulders. "What's that?"

"Alice over here has a new regular it seems." Amber wiggles her eyebrows at me.

Oh god. Can she tell how much this whole situation has rattled me? Her teasing tone seems to suggest so.

"And that regular customer just happens to be Jack Cleary?" Richard asks. "Well, I suppose it makes sense. I think he's from around here."

"Kingston," I mumble.

"Getting to know him already, I see! Are we sure he's just a customer and not an admirer?" Amber teases.

Her question stings. I hate how perceptive she can be. "Forget it, it's not like that!"

"Have you ever been to his restaurant? It's quite something," Richard asks.

"It's a bit out of my price range," I remark dryly.

Amber looks at him with an expectant smile on her face. "Maybe Alice here can get us a reservation, what do you think?"

"Calm down, will you? I barely know the man," I

grumble. *Unfortunately.*

"And yet… He's been doing your homework for you," she observes.

"One time! I don't even know if I'll ever see him again after interrupting his coffee break with my dumb questions." I bite my bottom lip and look away. That's not entirely true, I guess. I could always call him to ask for more help… He did offer. God, I hope we'll meet again. He really is something special, as my racing heart and butterflies in my stomach seek to remind me whenever I think of him.

"I don't buy it. There's more to this story," Amber says.

Richard chuckles and shakes his head. "Ah, let her be. She'll tell you everything whenever she's ready."

I shoot a grateful smile in Richard's direction. I will. Just as soon as I know what the hell is going on in my own head or heart! Because at this point, the only thing I do know is, I'm sleep deprived and confused, and I'm not even sure if half the things I remember from yesterday are real or just figments of my own wishful thinking.

But then again, that business card he gave me, which supposedly has his personal number and email address on it: I definitely didn't imagine that. Neither did I imagine the delicious scent of his cologne, still clinging to it…

Just like that, I'm distracted again.

CHAPTER FIVE

* Jack *

It's been a productive day. To reward myself, I've settled down in the conservatory. My favorite chair, perfect view overlooking the gardens where the late summer flowers are still blooming, and a glass of cognac in hand.

After meetings with the lawyers as well as Albert, my long-suffering financial advisor, I've worked out that it would indeed be feasible for me to invest in Alice's coffee shop business as a silent partner. However...

How do I even broach the topic with her? And how will her banker boyfriend react to the situation? She's a beautiful young woman. It might seem suspicious that I'm taking such an interest in her venture. Will he feel threatened? I would, if I were in his shoes. I would think I'm a creep and rightly so.

Admittedly, my motives aren't entirely pure. Even if I would never intrude on another relationship. There's just something about her which makes me want to seek her out. Again and again. Being around her has made me feel a side to me which I didn't know I had. She makes me want to be a better man. Kinder; more patient.

It took a lot of restraint to skip past Coffee to the Rescue on the way to my various meetings of the day. Enough is enough. I can't keep going there under the guise of getting coffee every single day, sometimes twice. That would be undignified.

So, what would I do if this were any other business deal? I would have Carrie reach out and set up a meeting. Either at my office, or maybe even at the law firm. But Alice doesn't have the faintest idea who Carrie is, and it would be such a copout not to talk to her directly.

Decisions, decisions.

I take a sip of cognac, and enjoy the smooth yet rich aromas of citrus and ginger as they swirl around in my mouth. It's a treat, which I afford myself every so often after a long day. Sometimes none other than my trusty *L'Or de Jean Martell* will do. Merely catching sight of the beautifully crafted bottle is a joy. The contents are on a whole other level of perfection. Just the right thing to put me in the mood for quiet introspection.

Will she accept my offer, once I decide to reach out to her? It's hardly the kind of thing you suggest over a phone call, or a rushed conversation at a busy coffee shop.

Perhaps we ought to discuss it over a proper meal. I'll make it clear that's all this is. A business deal. A helping hand, to get her situated on her feet, with a healthy upside for me should things work out, so it doesn't come across as charity. Not just a quick and dirty plaster to soothe the guilt I've felt ever since I found out I'll be displacing her charming little coffee shop. Even if she is just the manager. And it's certainly not an attempt to intrude on her existing relationship or life.

I would never.

Then again, if I was being entirely fair, I should be making similar plans with the lady running the art gallery next door, shouldn't I? And I'm not. Perhaps because I haven't gotten to know her? And I don't know the first thing about her business model either, so I wouldn't be of much help.

In any case, I can't finance every small business out of my own pocket. But I can try to support Alice… I hope she'll still see it that way, especially by the time the truth comes out. With a bit of luck and tactful handling of the situation, she won't hold my omissions against me. If we're going to partner on this venture, I'm going to need to have her trust.

I'm still planning my next moves, when my phone rings, startling me out of my daydream. Alice? Who else even has this number, except Carrie? And she knows not to disturb me after hours unless it's an emergency.

I'm almost disappointed, yet also strangely relieved when I see a different name on the screen.

"Sean. Hey…" I answer.

"Jack, hope I haven't caught you at an inconvenient time?"

I lean back in my chair and enjoy another sip of cognac. "Just enjoying a hard-earned drink after a long day…"

"I hear ya. Seems like we've both inherited the workaholic gene from Dad, huh?"

"Have we? I always figured you got more of the drinking gene, since I'm the only one of us who's ever worked a *real* job…" I tease. The job thing is an old topic between us. One which we can laugh about now, in hindsight.

He chuckles. "Ah, that was just a phase. Plus, I'm not the one drinking alone right now."

I raise my glass at the serene view out the window. "Well then, don't leave me hanging and pour yourself a glass too." I catch myself smiling and realize I'm actually glad Sean called. After years or little to no contact between us, he was the one who reached out first, only a few weeks ago. And we've fallen into a comfortable dynamic of mutual leg-pulling, interspersed with actual, deeper conversation. It felt alien at first, but I've come to enjoy it by now. I used to see him as my misguided little brother, but he's certainly grown up a lot over the years.

"What's going on with you, anyway?" I ask. "How's the missus?"

He sighs deeply before answering. "Things are really good, actually. That's what I'm calling about."

"Oh yeah?"

"Yeah. Ever since that cluster fuck with the tabloids—"

"And your epic comeback monologue during your last comedy special—"

"Yep, that. Well, honestly…" He goes quiet for a moment, and I hear the familiar sound of liquid pouring into a glass. "Cheers, Jack."

"Cheers."

"Lily is the best thing that's ever happened to me." Sean's voice is solemn now. Completely serious. And totally unlike him.

"I'm glad to hear it," I say. Strangely, I mean it. I didn't know what to think when I read the coverage in the papers about their affair. My little brother, photographed with a girl young enough to be his daughter. Totally inappropriate. Plus, the tabloids made things worse by digging up an old picture of her in a school uniform and printing it alongside a very unflattering shot of him.

Then again, how would I know not to judge him? We've had a difficult history. I'd spent my twenties and thirties working my ass off to build up first a career as a fine dining chef, then a television career on top of it. Meanwhile, Sean never grew out of being the class clown, or so it seemed.

Sure, he made a name for himself in the comedy circuit, but scandal after scandal kept following him around, making me wonder how long the TV networks would put up with his nonsense. Now, it seems my kid brother has finally landed on his feet. All thanks to a twenty-something girl from a rough part of town named Lily. Life can be funny sometimes.

"She's the one, Jack," Sean remarks, after taking a sip.

"How?" I wonder aloud. "How do you know?"

"She brings out a side to me which I never knew I had. In my previous relationships, I never had the patience to look outside myself. To see another perspective. It was like Mom and Dad all over again, but now—"

"Lily makes you want to be a better man," I conclude. Funny. That's just what I was thinking about in relation to Alice.

"She really does."

"It's not really fair, is it?"

"What is?" Sean asks.

"That we behave like absolute dickheads on our own, making a mess of our personal lives along the way, until some girl comes along who—" I'm not even sure I'm talking about Sean anymore with this statement. Too much has happened in my own past to be able to point fingers at anyone else.

"Who changes everything? Yeah, it probably isn't. But I'm glad it happened anyway," Sean concludes.

"Yeah. I suppose I'm being too cynical, as usual."

"Don't go soft on me now, or you'll get fired from your cushy cooking competition job!" Sean warns.

I let out a deep laugh. Yeah, he's right. I probably would. I'm the perpetual villain, and the producers as well as the audience love it.

"Anyway, so I called up to say that we'd love to have you over for dinner one day soon. Lily wants to meet you, and I obviously would love for you two to meet as well."

I nod thoughtfully. Makes sense, considering how serious they appear to have become.

"Any time, Sean."

"We'll have it catered, though. Because although she's been trying, bless her, Lily isn't feeling up to the job of having a chef of your caliber taste her cooking."

I grin. That's probably fair enough. "How about I host you guys instead?" I suggest. "We could meet up at the Kingston restaurant?"

"Ah, she wanted it to be something informal, at our place… I'll discuss it with her and let you know the details."

"Whatever you guys decide," I say.

There's a short pause. "Hey, Jack?"

"Yep?"

"Everything alright? I've never known you to be this agreeable," Sean says.

"Oh, I've just had a lot on my mind… Plans for the new restaurant, you understand." Not so much the restaurant, more the coffee shop currently in its place. Or rather, the person who works at said coffee shop. Who is making me more agreeable as per Sean. Jesus. If it's that obvious how she's affected me over a brief phone call, then I really am in trouble.

"Alright well, I'll be in touch then," Sean says.

"Sure thing, have a good one, Sean." I pause. "Uhh, actually, are you still there?"

"Yep. What's going on?" Sean asks.

"So… There's a girl."

I can hear Sean's low chuckle on the other end of the line. "I knew it! Since when has opening a new restaurant ever fazed my big brother? There had to be something else at play."

"Yeah, yeah," I grumble, but I'm not actually annoyed with him for a change.

"So, what's the trouble?"

My first instinct is to ask why he's jumping to conclusions about there being trouble, but I check myself. He's not exactly wrong. A deep breath later, I tell him all about what's been going on. From the first morning I entered Alice's shop to the proposal I've drawn up with the lawyers.

"Yeah…" Sean sounds unusually thoughtful. But then, he's been doing that a lot lately. "It's great that you're trying to rescue her, and I'm sure your intentions are good."

I suppress a cough.

"But one thing I've learned about women is that you've got to communicate. You can't make assumptions or keep them in the dark and expect them to appreciate you for it when you do come clean."

"Right. I plan to talk to her."

"You had to come clean yesterday, so to speak," Sean says.

I frown. "But I hadn't finalized the plan yet."

"My point exactly, you needed to involve her in the planning. Anyway. Can't change the past, only the future. Talk to her as soon as possible. And for God's sake, tell her what she means to you as well."

That's… If I tell her how I feel about her, she'll never want to enter into a business deal with me! Or at least it will create immeasurable tension between her and her man. I can't have that on my conscience, can I? Maybe Sean hasn't wised up as much as I thought.

"I'll think about it," I grumble.

"Okay. Break a leg, big brother."

I hang up the phone and empty my glass with one final sip. That's it. I have decided the right course forward, no matter what Sean is trying to tell me. Because he's obviously wrong.

First thing in the morning, I'm personally calling up Alice to invite her to dinner to discuss my proposal and my proposal *only*. It's the proper thing to do, and will ensure she's amenable to accepting my help after all the trouble I've already caused her. I'll tell her the whole, unadulterated truth about the situation with her landlord, and I'll leave the paperwork with her. That way, she and her banker boyfriend can look it over in peace and satisfy themselves that it's indeed a good deal for everyone involved. And we'll take it from there. After that, the ball will be in her court, and I can rest easy, knowing I've done everything possible to make things right.

What I will *not* do, however, is take my little brother's advice about declaring any kind of *feelings* for her, because that'll muddy the waters. She's in a relationship already, and she's facing a lot of professional instability. The last thing she needs is for me to intrude on her status quo any more than I've already done.

And even otherwise, between this restaurant project, my TV career, and mentoring her in her coffee shop business, I have neither the time nor mental capacity to think about dating. Plus, she's way too young for me, so she'd never see me in that light anyway. So what if I spend every waking moment dreaming of her beautiful smile? I'll suck it up and carry on. Expressing these idle fantasies will only cause unnecessary pain. For everyone involved.

I sigh deeply and crack my knuckles, trying to release some of the tension I've been carrying around with me over the last couple of days. It works, only somewhat. At least I have a plan now. Still, that lingering sense of guilt doesn't quite leave me be. Perhaps it was naive of me to expect it to. It probably won't, not until I've told her the truth, our partnership is formalized, and Alice and her coffee shop business have landed on their feet.

CHAPTER SIX

*** Alice ***

My morning starts like any other. I'm not quite as shattered as yesterday, but I'm not 100% alert either. That's probably why it takes me a full five seconds to understand what I'm hearing when I answer the coffee shop landline at nine sharp in the morning. I'm half expecting a junk call. Or maybe someone from one of the shops and offices nearby to place a takeaway order.

The last thing I expect is Jack's deep, sexy voice, asking me if I'm busy tonight.

"Umm, no," I finally say. I'm never busy at night. Is he asking me out? Am I hallucinating?

"I'd like to discuss something important with you. In private," he says.

That doesn't quite answer the millions of questions my brain is throwing my way.

"And so I wanted to propose a quiet dinner. At my restaurant," he continues.

Dinner with Jack-fucking-Cleary at his perpetually booked fancy pants restaurant. Holy shit.

"If it's okay with you, that is."

Okay? It's bloody perfect, and yet…

"Of course. I'd love to join you for dinner," I hear myself say. Thankfully I sound a lot more confident than I feel.

"Would eight be okay? What time do you shut shop?" he asks.

"Eight is perfect. Should I meet you there?" Not that I know where the hell 'there' is exactly. But I'm sure Google Maps can handle the logistics.

"I'll send a car?" he asks.

So that's how the other half live. Fancy!

"Uhh, okay…"

"If it's not too forward, might I have your mobile number so we can coordinate?" Jack asks.

"Oh, yeah, of course." I quickly rattle off my digits.

"Great, I'll see you tonight at eight, then."

"Cool, yeah. It's a date," I mumble.

There's an awkward pause on the other end, which just about makes me lose my mind. Did I really just say that? Was that not his intention? I'm about to start hyperventilating with nerves, when he clears his throat and says: "I'm looking forward to it. See you tonight, Alice."

And relief washes over me immediately. I lower the receiver and just try to breathe.

Holy shit. He asked me to dinner. And although

he didn't define it as such, he also didn't correct me. That means, it *is* a date? Or it could turn into one? Or…

I hang up the phone properly, cover my mouth with both hands, and squeal as loud as I can.

Just then, the door chime goes off and Amber and Richard walk in.

"Morning, Alice!" they speak in unison.

I'm still breathing heavily when I reciprocate. "Morning!"

"Everything alright? You look like you've just seen a—" Richard starts.

"Was it Jack Cleary? It was, wasn't it?" Amber starts looking around the shop, as if she's expecting to find him hidden under a table or something.

I shake out both my hands and arms and wipe my clammy palms on my apron. "He just phoned the shop. Cos, you know, he doesn't—didn't—actually have my cell…"

"Ohhh!" Amber wiggles her eyebrows expectantly. "And, what did he want?"

"He wants to have dinner. With me!" I say.

"That's great! When?"

My throat closes up and my chest feels heavy when I respond. "Tonight."

"Wonderful! I'm so happy for you!" Amber grins widely.

I want to agree, because it is a dream come true, in

a way. Hopefully the start of one of those really explicit ones I've been having lately. But it's also a complete nightmare.

"Jesus Christ, what the fuck do I even wear?" I exclaim while trying to shake the nervous energy out of my hands.

Amber presses her lips together and stares at me.

"Yes, well… Okay, that's a good point. I can definitely help you decide, if you wanna head home real quick and show me what you've got."

I gesture wildly at my surroundings. "I can't leave here! It's just about to get busy! And also, I pretty much don't own anything other than jeans and t-shirts."

"When's Deedee coming in?" Amber asks.

I try to breathe. "At two."

"Then we'll go shopping as soon as she gets here. Richard, sweetheart, you don't mind if I leave you alone this afternoon, do you?"

He suppresses a smile and shakes his head. "You both go ahead and do what you need to do."

I exhale sharply. "Okay." A few deep breaths later, and I feel my anxiety wane. "Good idea. Yes. Okay."

"This is so exciting, though!" Amber squeals.

A few deep breaths later and yes, I can finally agree. "I can't believe he asked me to dinner. Holy shit!" I mumble. This time when I say it, a smile creeps over my face. A bright, infectious smile, which makes my chest feel all warm inside and which lingers for the rest of the morning.

***

It's just after two when I leave Deedee to manage the shop and head out with Amber in tow as my style guru. When we made our shopping plan this morning, Lauren's little boutique around the corner was the only logical destination we came up with. She's a designer specializing in curvy sizes, as well as a friend and coffee shop regular. Sure, her clothes are on the expensive end of the scale, but if I'm going to impress a man as sophisticated as Jack Cleary, I can't do it with cheap, disposable fashion.

Ordinarily, I would have scoffed at the idea of spending so much on an outfit, and worried about my monthly budget. But it's been so long since I've purchased anything for myself, I barely recall the experience. You don't get a lot of opportunities to splurge at the shops, when you're always working at your own.

Married to the work already, as Jack had warned during our last conversation. Was he dropping a hint about his intentions? I certainly hope so. Maybe our date is going to be a step in the right direction. Ugh. So much for not getting my hopes up too soon!

I do wonder what mysterious thing he wants to discuss with me over dinner. He sounded so secretive about it on the phone, and I don't know him well enough to give in to my impulse to pry further. Luckily the wait isn't too long and I'll find out in a few hours.

"Hey!" Lauren greets us. "Aren't you two a sight for sore eyes?"

"Lauren! Business must have picked up lately, I barely see you around the coffee shop these days," I tell her. "I've taken the liberty of bringing you over one of those caramel cappuccinos you like so much."

She accepts the pink and white dotted takeaway cup with a bright smile. "You're an angel, thanks! And Amber, I've been planning to call you to reach out to some fashion influencers for me, but it's been a chore trying to get the designs for the winter collection finalized, so I haven't had the chance…"

"No problem. I'll still be here once you get it all sorted out," Amber says.

Lauren takes the cap off her drink and takes a deep whiff. "So good. I really needed this."

Amber and I stand around in silence while she takes a sip. I'm already scanning the displays from the corner of my eye. Where do I even start? This might just be harder than I thought.

"Sooo," Lauren starts, while scrutinizing both of us. "I'm guessing this isn't purely a social call?"

I awkwardly shuffle from one foot to the other.

"We're here for an outfit to make our dear Alice

look like a million bucks," Amber jumps in.

Lauren smiles brightly. "Oh, well *that* I can certainly help with. Not that Alice doesn't already look beautiful as is, but you get what I'm saying."

I smile, but can't bring myself to look up and make eye contact with either of them right now. Because I'm expecting it. The very obvious and very inevitable question.

"Any special occasion?" Lauren asks.

There it is. And I still don't know how to answer. The silence that follows is deafening. Until Amber takes over. "Well, you'll never guess who asked our dear Alice out."

"Amber, please!" I interject. However, if I'm really honest, I do feel a little proud. Or flattered. Or I don't know how to describe what I feel. It's probably just the nerves of going on a date for the first time in so long.

"Is it someone I know?" Lauren asks excitedly. "Ohh, is it someone famous, by any chance?"

I'm still shaking my head, but Amber can't contain her excitement and is grinning from ear to ear now.

"I'd say so. Wouldn't you say so, Alice?"

"I…"

"Don't leave me hanging now. One of you two better tell me everything!" Lauren complains.

"Well, you've already said everything else. You might as well be the one to—" I turn to Amber, who doesn't require much more prompting from me or Lauren, because she simply can't contain herself any longer.

"It's Jack Cleary. The chef!" she exclaims.

My heart is racing. My cheeks are getting warmer by the second. And I don't know where to look anymore.

Lauren turns to me, smiling brightly. "Wow! I mean… I've always thought he was hot… Don't get me wrong, but like… in a domineering kind of way? Like he seems very—"

"He's much nicer in person than on TV," I reassure her. Or myself.

"So he just came into the coffee shop the other morning. I caught a glimpse of him as he was leaving," Amber says. "Apparently he's local to this area."

"Ohh! Well, now, ladies, allow me to spill some tea…" Lauren leans in with a knowing smile.

"Yes, please!" Amber says.

I'm not sure where this is going, but the temptation proves too much, even for me. Any additional information about my date is bound to be helpful.

"You guys know how Lawrence is a pretty big deal in real estate, right?"

"Right," Amber and I reply simultaneously. Lauren's boyfriend's company owns half the buildings on this block, including the one we're standing in right now. Along with many more across London.

"So he was telling me a few weeks ago that he's been in touch with Jack Cleary's people about finding a suitable location for a new restaurant…"

Sure… makes sense. His restaurants are always booked months in advance. Of course he'd be looking to expand his business.

"And he did try, and one of Lawrence's properties around here seemed to be what he was looking for, but in the end the whole thing fell through. Apparently some no-name nobody who only owns like two buildings in town made the deal."

"Wow! So he's been looking at property nearby for a restaurant? How exciting!" Amber chirps. "This area is really picking up!"

"Yeah… super exciting," I mumble. Could it be? It would be too big a coincidence not to…

The nobody Lauren referred to must be my old boss's son… And Jack's chosen location for his new restaurant is… the current location of Coffee for the Rescue. As well as the art gallery next door. That explains so much.

"Umm…" Lauren turns to me with a concerned frown on her face. "Are you okay, Alice?"

"Just peachy, thanks," I say, while straightening myself. So that's the big secret he wanted to discuss with me. He's been hanging around the coffee shop, not because he suddenly developed a taste for my medium roast or has any interest in me personally, but because he's been checking out the location. He's probably already drawing up plans for all the renovation work he intends to carry out once I'm shut down.

And he's helping me with my business plan, because… Well, I wonder why, actually. Guilty conscience? What the hell do I do now? Go along with our dinner plans and pretend I don't know what's going on? Or tell him where to shove his guilty conscience and cancel?

I wander away from Lauren and Amber, who are still chatting away, brushing my fingertips against the luxurious fabrics of the pretty dresses lining the wall of Lauren's boutique. Each piece is even better than the last. With a price tag to match.

I'd feel like a million bucks in any one of these. Maybe, if I explain the situation, Lauren will let me borrow one, just to show Jack-fucking-Cleary everything he's missing out on. Only for ten minutes. Just long enough to make my point, and then she can have it back, tag and all. No harm no foul.

No, that's pathetic too.

"Alice? Seriously. Something is wrong, don't you try to deny it." Amber puts her hand on my shoulder, prompting me to turn around.

I make a face and shake my head. "I can't be 100%

sure, but…" I look over at Lauren, who's silently observing the two of us from a few steps further away.

"I think he's the reason I'm getting shut down. That's why he came in on Monday morning, just when I got the letter from my landlord. And why he's been returning again and again. When he asked me out to dinner over the phone, he told me he had something to discuss with me and was acting all mysterious about it. It would be too big a coincidence for it to be anything else. I think Jack only asked me out for dinner tonight to tell me he's taking over the lease on the coffee shop."

"Oh shit. And that's why he's been looking at your business plan as well. Because he felt bad about the position he's putting you in?" Amber says.

I nod. "I think so."

Lauren covers her mouth with her hand and just stares at me. "You're getting shut down? I had no idea. Crap, I'm so sorry."

"It's all happened so quickly, I haven't had the chance to talk to anyone about this yet. But I'm so glad you told me what you know. At least this way, I'm walking into the situation prepared."

"Alice, sweetie…" Amber puts her arm around me. "I think our mission here has changed. And yet it also hasn't changed at all."

"How so?"

"We have to find you the perfect dress so that you can knock him dead just before you tell him to fuck off."

"But…" I stammer. But what if it was never meant to be a date? What if it was literally *just* dinner?

"I can't believe I'm saying this, but…" Lauren says, joining me and putting her hand on my other shoulder. "I'm totally with Amber on this. We're going to get you the perfect dress, get your hair done, and your make-up. You're going to turn up to dinner looking totally stunning, and he's going to spend the rest of his life regretting ever screwing you over like this. Nobody fucks over our Alice and gets away with it."

"But…" I close my eyes and think back to the interactions we've shared over the past week. The little smiles, the stares, the patience and kindness he showed me, which seemed to be a side of him which he doesn't share with anyone. At least not in front of the camera, or in any media appearance I've ever seen.

Did he really screw me over like Lauren says? After all, we only met for the first time mere hours before the letter informing me of my coffee shop's closure arrived. That means the deal was already done by then. He didn't know what or who was occupying the building he signed a contract on. It wasn't anything personal. If anyone's to blame, it should be the landlord, who didn't even give me a chance to take over the shop myself.

Do I really need to dress up to the nines for tonight, to do what—take some kind of petty revenge on Jack by leading him on and then rejecting him? Isn't that just a bit too juvenile?

Because, hell, I hate that he's hidden this information from me so far, but I… I really do like him, still. The way my heart and body reacted every moment we spent together, however innocuous. The way he's been on my mind every night and every morning. The little surge of pride I felt when Lauren admitted she's always found him attractive too…

I'm not hurt because he's planning to open a restaurant in what for all intents and purposes has been my little coffee shop so far. Okay, I am a little hurt. But mostly, I'm hurt because I wanted tonight's dinner to be an actual date. And now I'm thinking that perhaps it's not. Perhaps it's just his way of softening the blow before telling me the truth.

Perhaps he never really noticed me the way I noticed him.

Perhaps all those little smiles and looks were just that. Innocent smiles. Meaningless looks. Just him trying to be nice for a change.

What if I got my hopes up for nothing? Maybe this isn't the start of my epic love story, but just another day in the life of Alice. Boring wannabe coffee shop owner who will never find true love, least of all with a successful, sophisticated man like Jack Cleary. What if it was all an idle fantasy?

"Come on, chin up. We've got this," Lauren tells me, squeezing my shoulder.

Amber nods. "Give us an hour or two. We'll get you ready like Cinderella for the ball."

"Right. We'll be your fairy godsisters. If there is such a thing."

"You guys…" I say. But I don't know how to end that statement. 'You shouldn't have?'

Who knows. Maybe this is exactly what my bruised ego needs.

CHAPTER SEVEN

* Jack *

The moment Alice enters the private dining suite I'd reserved for tonight, I struggle to remember my good intentions for the evening. This is not a business dinner dress she's wearing. It's a date dress. Or perhaps even an affair dress.

She has pulled out all the stops when getting ready for tonight. I already thought she was gorgeous in her everyday role as barista, with her cute little nametag and apron draped over form-fitting jeans. But now… I forget why I was trying to act professional in the first place.

It's hopeless.

The satiny fabric drapes around her curves like fondant on a wedding cake. Her tasteful makeup and hair complement the classy look. Delicious, sensuous perfection. Her entire persona has changed too; it's obvious she knows exactly how good she looks as she strides towards me with her head held high.

Boyfriend or no boyfriend, my moral compass has stopped working and all the needles are pointing at her. And everything I planned to tell her last night has suddenly lost its meaning.

The only question on my mind is how much better she'd look naked and spread across the satin sheets on my bed.

"Hi…" she says, with a subtle smile playing on her lips.

"Alice… Wow," I hear myself say, while greeting her with a half-hug.

Very smooth. Grand job. I'm despicable.

She doesn't respond, because why on earth would she? That wasn't even a compliment, that was just daft. Bloody hell. Words; what are those?

I clear my throat and try to focus. "You look absolutely stunning."

Her smile brightens and she even blushes a little while averting her gaze. Though as soon as I said that, I realized what an understatement it was. She looks delicious enough to eat. I can't very well tell her that, though…

"It's not every day you get invited to a fancy dinner by a Michelin star chef…" she mumbles, glancing up at me through thick black lashes.

Is that what this is? Is she simply star struck? No way… She wasn't nearly this flustered the last time we met. Or when we spoke over the phone in the morning. She's been perfectly composed throughout our interactions so far, but now… I can't put my finger on what has changed exactly, and yet everything is different tonight.

"Please, take a seat." I pull out a chair for her and nearly lose my sense of balance when I deeply inhale her subtle perfume. Sweet like the cinnamon rolls she serves in her cafe, but oh so seductive too…

"Thanks so much for the dinner invitation, Jack," she says, while taking a seat.

My chest swells with all kinds of unfamiliar sensations. I had planned to formalize a professional partnership with this woman, and now… That's the last thing on my mind. I *want* her. I want to do unspeakable things to her. But first of all, I wish to feed her. At least *that* I know how to do properly.

"Ah, don't mention it." I take a seat across from her and forget to breathe when her eyes settle on mine. Jesus Christ. I've forgotten how to converse, how to act, even how to *be*. And it's all down to her presence. "I'm glad you could make it. I was concerned that my invitation would be inappropriate…"

She frowns. "Inappropriate?"

"Well, in case your boyfriend—"

"I don't have a boyfriend," Alice interjects.

"The banker?"

"A regular customer and *my friend's* boyfriend." She smiles and leans forward just enough for my gaze to be drawn to her cleavage. That's it. The realization that she's single just about breaks my brain in half. Something in me snaps, and all memory of my plans for this conversation is wiped away.

"That's a relief," I say.

"Is it? How come?" she asks.

"Because I'd very much like a chance to apply for the job."

Her eyes widen as she exhales sharply through parted lips, which is the first little indicator she's giving me that the old Alice is still in there somewhere. The Alice who's in equal parts formidable and vulnerable. Who makes me admire her courage and want to be the source of it all at once.

That's some bullshit, though. Because I can't be that for anyone. I've only ever lived for myself: *my* ambitions, *my* dreams. What makes me think I have what it takes to be a source of support for anyone else?

Sean was right when he used the word workaholic. Somehow he's made the switch toward bettering himself and being in an actual relationship. But he's my kid brother, and we're nothing alike. Is it too late for me? Am I too set in my ways? Or is this yet another thing Alice can teach me about?

* Alice *

I had the best of intentions throughout the chauffeur drive to Kingston. Even as I arrived at the restaurant and was ushered towards a private dining room, my mission was clear. I was going to keep my composure and let Jack lead the conversation to find out what tonight is all about. I was going to hear him out, no matter how betrayed I'd felt that he might have been hiding his true intentions from me until now.

Who am I anyway? We were strangers to each other only a few days ago, and I can hardly make sweeping judgments about the man based on the very limited conversations we've shared so far. Who knows why he wanted me to meet him for dinner? No matter how badly I'd wanted it to be a date only hours ago, I wasn't going to push the issue.

And then I saw how he looked at me in the stunning dress Lauren and Amber picked out for me. My insides went weak and my resolve crumbled. The brief little hug he gave me as a greeting sent me flying over the edge of self control. Because I could feel his heat against me, and it brought all those forbidden dreams I've been having about him right back into focus.

"I don't have a boyfriend," I hear myself say. He says something about a banker, and I try my best to answer coherently.

"That's a relief." Jack's voice is even more gravelly

than normal.

I mumble something. My thoughts aren't making much sense to me right now.

"Because I'd very much like a chance to apply for the job," he says.

That's it. My brain has fused and taken all remnants of rational thought with it. Well, almost. I try to catch a breath, but it's proving difficult. My heart is racing out of control and my palms are so sweaty I barely know what to do with them. Thank god I'm sitting down, or I would have lost my balance for sure.

The way he's looking at me from across the table is something else. All I can do is stare back. And to think I've been agonizing over this moment all afternoon. Is it a date; is it not a date? This question has been well and truly answered. Well, unless this is a hookup and not a date, but at this point, I'm not sure me and my raging hormones care to make that kind of distinction. In this different setting, far away from the mundane everyday of the coffee shop, all logic has flown out the window for me. I don't care about anything anymore. I just know that I want this man, any way I can get him.

"Maybe, as we get to know each other over dinner, you'll—" he says.

"I'm not hungry," I blurt out.

He presses his lips together and continues to stare

deep into my soul. He must see the desperation. The animalistic need has to be radiating off me with every hurried breath.

"No?"

I shake my head. "Not unless you're the main course."

Yep. My brain is definitely broken. I can't believe I just said that. This isn't like me at all. I'm not this forward. I'm not this brazen. I could see someone like Amber or Lauren use these words. Those two own their femininity and sexuality. Not me. I'm boring old Alice, who is most at home plating up cinnamon rolls and pouring coffee. I don't proposition or seduce, what the hell am I thinking?

Oh yeah, I'm *not* thinking.

For a brief moment, a hint of a smile creeps across his face. He pushes his chair back, and I can't breathe. I can't do anything other than watch him approach me until he's towering over me. The tempting scent of his cologne is so obvious now, not like the mere hint I was getting from his business card earlier. It's delicious. *He's* delicious.

He continues to gaze down into my eyes while gently placing his hand on my cheek and brushes his thumb across my bottom lip.

"You're playing with fire…" he growls.

My eyelids flutter involuntarily. "I know," I whisper. Or try to, because I can't hear myself over the incessant thumping of my heart.

"I live nearby," he says. "We could…"

"Yes," I breathe. Yes, to whatever this is. Even if everything goes to shit by morning, this right here is still the most exciting thing to happen to me since… Ever. I'll be damned if I'm going to let the opportunity pass me by.

The moment we step out of the restaurant, Jack's hand finds mine, and we rush towards the waiting car. The cool evening air does nothing to dampen the heat between us. I can hardly focus on anything but the sweet anticipation of what's to come. The drive to his house is a blur of streetlights and shadows, as the tension between us builds with every passing second.

We don't *do* anything. Not yet. We don't even talk; we just hold hands. And even just the sensation of his large, warm hand holding onto mine is almost too much to bear. Despite the relative privacy of the secluded dining room back at the restaurant and the backseat of his car isn't enough to convince us to really let go. It's an unspoken rule between us. Nothing will happen until we're truly alone.

When the driver pulls up the driveway to a modern villa on the edge of town, I barely notice the grandeur. Frankly, I'm not even sure where exactly we are. My attention is consumed by the man beside me, his hand still firmly clasped in mine. Or vice versa. I exit the car in a hurry, looking back just in time to see him rushing behind me. His hand briefly rests on the small of my back as he walks me up the steps to the front door. There, Jack briefly shows me a glimpse of his own frazzled state of mind while he fumbles with his keys.

As soon as the door shuts behind us, the outside world is quickly forgotten. His hands are on me, sliding over the satiny fabric of my dress, pulling me closer. I can feel the heat of his body through the thin material, burning straight into my skin. Our mouths find each other, and for a moment I can breathe again. Because this is it. This is everything I tried not to fantasize about during the lead up to this. Our first kiss is deep and hungry, a promise of everything to come.

We stumble through the hallway, our lips barely parting, our hands exploring every inch of each other. God, he's so hot. So sure of himself. And I'm swept up in his force field, not just following his lead but also forging a path of exploration on my own. This is a dream which I've had repeatedly, and nothing about it disappoints.

The house is a blur of modern architecture and sleek design, but I don't care about any of it. All I care about is him, the way his touch sets my skin ablaze, the way his scent envelops me. How my fingertips graze across his torso, up to his broad shoulders. His body is firm beneath my touch, but not completely. He's all man. Real and hot blooded, with a physique to match. Whoever decided dad bods were in, I agree wholeheartedly. His tall stature and solid build exude strength and power. I'm not little by any means, but he makes me feel it anyway. Small and dainty, and totally at his mercy.

We barely make it up the steps to the bedroom, items of clothing scattering along the way. My shoes, at the bottom of the stairs, his coat and tie somewhere midway. His fingers pause on the zip of my dress, as if they're waiting for my permission. I don't speak; I've forgotten how. Instead, I start fumbling with the buttons on his shirt to signal my approval. He makes short work of my carefully curated outfit, and it falls to the floor in a puddle of satin.

Ordinarily, this is where I'd have a little moment. A change of heart, or at least a surge of nerves. But not with him. I stand before him, dressed only in my bra and panties, still feeling invincible.

"You're beautiful, Alice," he murmurs.

It's in his eyes, in his entire being. The way he admires me not just with his looks, but with his fingertips. Like I'm the gift he's always wanted, just as he is mine.

Now, this isn't my dream anymore. It's better.

He steps back, his gaze never leaving mine as he undresses the rest of the way. Each piece of clothing that falls away reveals more of him, and I can't help but marvel at the sight. He's gorgeous, flawless skin with just the right amount of hair accentuating his broad chest and belly.

"Beautiful," I agree, only to realize that no sound came out. I can only smile.

I can't believe this marvel of a man is all mine. Even if it is just for tonight. That'll do. This is going to be the one I'll remember forever. The night I did something crazy and got out of my own head and earned myself a piece of masculine perfection.

His hands find my hips, pulling me towards him, before laying me down on the bed. He gets on top of me, our bodies pressing together, skin against skin. I can feel the heat of him, the hardness of him, with just the right amount of softness too. Because he's a contradiction, this beautiful man with the silver hair and pale green eyes that could speak a thousand words in silence. His mouth finds mine again, and I cling on for dear life to stop myself from drowning.

His hands roam every inch of my body, tracing lines of fire over my skin. I arch into his touch, my body aching with need. His mouth follows the path of his hands, kissing and nipping, with the scratch of his beard driving me even wilder. I can't think, can't breathe, can only feel.

And it feels incredible.

I start to explore him too, my hands tracing the

muscles on his arms and shoulders, my mouth tasting the side of his neck. He groans under my affections, his body tensing as he struggles to practice restraint. It's a powerful feeling, knowing that I can affect him this way, and gives me the courage to touch more of him. This is the body of someone who enjoys a good meal, that much is clear. But he's not out of shape, far from it. He's just… Rich? Certainly decadent, and extremely delicious. I never thought about it much, but he's a perfect specimen of masculine beauty.

Just my type.

I run my hands across his chest, enjoying the tickle of his hair against my palm. There's so much pent up energy just simmering beneath the surface here, begging to be unleashed. He shudders with every touch. It's crazy to think I can make him feel as good as what he's doing to me.

"Playing with fire," he seems to growl under his breath, while I continue to tease. Until a change comes over him, and he lifts his head, staring straight into my soul. "Tell me stop and I will try."

I defiantly shake my head. "Never."

He grabs my wrists and raises them over my head, then he lowers himself onto me. His patience has run out, and so has mine. When he enters me, it's with a slow, deliberate thrust that takes my breath away. He fills me completely, our bodies fitting together like they were made for this. We move together, our rhythm perfectly matched, our bodies in sync. It's intense and overwhelming, a sensation unlike anything I've ever felt.

His eyes never leave mine, the connection between us deepening with every thrust, every touch, every kiss. I see myself reflected in his gaze, and I marvel at the woman I see. She's confident, powerful, sexy. She's everything I never thought I could be but somehow am with him.

The pleasure builds, a wave of sensation that threatens to overwhelm me. I cling to him, my nails digging into his back, my body tensing as I approach the edge. He's right there with me, his body shaking with the effort of holding back.

"Let go," he whispers, his voice barely audible. "Let go with me."

And I do. With a final, powerful thrust, we both go tumbling over the edge, our bodies convulsing with pleasure, our cries echoing in the quiet room. It's intense and overwhelming, a sensation unlike anything I've ever felt. And then, moments later, I'm overwhelmed yet again as his arms close around me, his body absorbs me into a comforting embrace, and I can finally breathe a sigh of profound relief.

"I'm sorry, it's been a good long while," he seems to whisper. I bury my face in his beard and fill my lungs with his scent and smile. If I wasn't certain of it before, I am now. Here in his arms, I'm safe. I am home.

The main event may not have lasted all that long, but that's okay. Because we do it again and again just to remind ourselves of its glory.

I already know that the memories of tonight will linger… forever.

CHAPTER EIGHT

Jack

I fucked up. There's no nicer way to describe it. As I look at Alice's sleeping form in the bed beside me, I'm consumed by more of that same feeling that's been haunting me since the day we met.

Guilt.

It *is* guilt. Always was.

I asked her to have dinner with me, to discuss a business proposal, for Pete's sake. None of this was even on my mind, so how did we end up here? Lying side by side, cuddling until she dozed off.

I lie; it was on my mind all along, I just wasn't planning on acting on it. And Alice... Sweet, gorgeous, perfect-in-every-way Alice caught onto my hidden desires and unleashed everything I had tried so hard to suppress. Because she thought this was a *date*.

And now, rather than business partners, I don't know what we are. And she still doesn't know the truth. Sean was right. I needed to come clean first. Not just about the business side of things, but about my feelings for her too. As the events of the past few hours have demonstrated, there was no way I could keep my attraction for her under control. It was doable to play it cool in a public setting, but alone with her? No fucking way. She needed to know everything in order to make an informed decision about how to move forward. And I probably shouldn't be investing in her coffee shop in the first place. Because in order to get into business with someone, you need clarity and perspective. I have neither when it comes to her.

What has the world come to, when my fuck-up little brother turns out to be the wise one? Well, I suppose he has more relationship experience than I do. Even if all of them failed spectacularly until now.

And that's exactly what I'm anticipating here. A burning train wreck. Once she finds out what's really going on, she'll be so hurt that she'll never want to see me again. I betrayed her trust and now I'm in too deep. I should have corrected her in the morning, when she referred to our dinner appointment as a date. I should have—

I rest my head in my hands and try to focus. Nothing fazes me normally. Put me in a kitchen during dinner service with everything going wrong all at once and I'll be the calmest guy in there. Contract negotiations with difficult suppliers or even TV execs; no problem. Carrie likes to refer to it as my 'psycho

Zen' state, which is actually rather offensive as well as amusing because it feels so apt. But now? There's nothing Zen about this situation. I'm spinning out of control and don't know how to reel myself back in. This right here—watching her sleep peacefully in my bed after we just did unspeakable things to each other—might never happen again now.

That thought is enough to break me all over again.

I carefully get up, trying not to wake her. Before long, I find myself in the same place as the last time I needed to think something through. The conservatory. I mindlessly pour myself a glass of cognac to take the edge off and sit back in my chair. The view out the window isn't like it was that evening. There are no colorful late summer blooms to soothe my frazzled nerves, just outlines of skeletal stalks and their shadows, dancing eerily in the moonlight as if to mock me.

I take a first big sip and immediately set the glass back down. Even this isn't the same. The realization of just how badly I messed up has left a bitterness in my mouth which I can't shake. Is this what it's going to be like? I hardly had a taste of a life with Alice, but is this what it's going to be like *without?*

I shake my head at myself. I'm better than this. I'm better than letting emotion overwhelm me. Perhaps I can still salvage things; explain myself to her. If only I can get some perspective.

I reach for my phone, which I'd mindlessly picked up on my way here. It's three in the morning. Absolutely not the time to be making calls. Still, he picks up within a couple of rings, flat. I put the phone to my ear and grab my glass again.

"Jack? Is everything okay?" Sean sounds out of breath.

"I'm afraid I didn't take your advice, little brother."

"No?" he asks. I hear a muffled female voice on the other end as well, but can't make out what she's saying. Poor Lily. I must have woken her up too.

"I should have… I planned to. Then she turned up to our dinner meeting looking like—"

Sean remains silent, allowing me to finish.

"One thing led to another, and now I'm in too deep, and we didn't exactly get the chance to do much talking."

"So what you're trying to say is: she likes you too. That's not so bad then."

I frown and shake my head. "You're not getting me."

There's another muffled exchange on the other end of the line. Fuck, can Lily hear everything I'm saying? I haven't even met the girl yet, and she must already think the worst of me.

"We have chemistry, sure, but because I didn't tell her the truth before we—you get the idea. It's a betrayal of trust. She's bound to feel hurt, and—"

"Jack, Jack, Jack," Sean interjects. That's exactly the tone I would use with him whenever he did something idiotic back in our younger days. Back before we lost touch for so many years. I hate that he's using it on me now. "Why are you talking to me right now, when the person you need to talk to is—Is she still at your place?"

I instinctively glance at the open sliding door leading out of the conservatory. My mind must be playing tricks on me, because for a brief moment, I think I see a shadow. Surely not. The bedroom is literally on the other end of the house, and she was sleeping soundly when I left her only minutes ago. There's no way she could have heard me talk and followed me.

"Yeah… She's here. But it's too late. I fucked up," I mumble, distracted by my own imagination.

"I can't believe I have to tell you this, but go talk to *her*. Not me. Not your therapist—"

I scoff at his mention of a therapist. As if.

"Go tell the girl—" Sean pauses at another interruption on his end. "Sorry, go tell the lady everything. Right now. Before you fuck things up any further."

I pinch the bridge of my nose and close my eyes. "Yeah." So this is what it feels like to eat humble pie. "You're right."

"And don't act all cool and stoic like you usually do, Jack! Tell her *everything* in detail. Especially the embarrassing mushy shit."

"Yeah," I mumble. Humble pie, indeed. "Thanks, Sean."

With that, I put the phone down. When I look up at the entrance to the conservatory again, I see her. Not a shadow, or a figment of my imagination. But Alice, wearing my button-down shirt like a robe, with her arms wrapped tightly around herself. Her dejected expression hurts like a dagger to the heart.

"Fuck," I curse under my breath. "You heard all that?"

* Alice *

When I wake up alone in Jack's bed, it takes me a minute to find my bearings. I go to the bathroom, and then I decide to explore the rest of the house. Surely he hasn't left me here all alone? And if he did, what does *that* mean? Does he regret what happened between us?

He didn't seem to in the moment, but then... I'm not entirely sure how much of what has transpired between us has been due to my own wishful thinking. I've been attracted to him since our first meeting, pretty much.

Jack... He hasn't been very forthcoming about his feelings on the matter, and I pretty much steered the entire encounter from the moment I arrived at his restaurant. Maybe he just got swept up in the moment, and now he's had his fun, and wishes I'd disappear already. I mean, I did pretty much throw myself at him at the very first opportunity. And once we'd had a few rounds of fun, I dozed off in his arms, leaving us no time to discuss things. The exhaustion of the past week has gotten to me, clearly.

I make my way around his very fancy, very modern, and very spacious house. Heading down the stairs, I move from one immaculately furnished room to the other, until I hear something in the distance.

Before long, I follow his muffled voice and find myself lingering at the open doorway of what looks to be a winter garden.

"She's here… It's too late," he says with a sigh. "I fucked up."

My heart sinks. *Too late. Fucked up.* So he *is* regretting everything that happened. On top of that, he's over there telling someone all the details. I feel cheap and more than a little dirty.

I got swept up in the moment and made myself too available; I should have known better, but—

All my instincts tell me to run, grab my clothes and get the hell out of his house before he has to tell me to, but… Something is stopping me. Because I might be boring old Alice from the coffee shop, who isn't quite as courageous and empowered as she thought she was an hour or so ago. But I'm no coward either. I'm not just going to slink out of here in my expensive designer dress to do the walk of shame to the night bus home. It takes two to tango, and he was tangoing pretty hard along with me earlier.

No. Screw it. I'm better than this.

I turn around again and position myself in the doorway, waiting with bated breath for Jack's rather one-sided conversation to end so we can talk. Like adults. It's the least we can do.

It doesn't take long. He puts the phone down, empties his glass, and spots me just as he's about to get up from his chair.

"Fuck. You heard all that?"

I press my lips together, but I'm screaming internally. Yes, I fucking heard enough, thank-you-very-much.

"If you wanted me to leave, after... you could have just said so, rather than pretend-cuddling with me."

He shakes his head. "No, no, no."

"Unless it took you a while to realize you'd fucked up by inviting me back here?"

He groans and runs his hand through his beard. It makes a delicious scratchy sound which gives me goose bumps. How is it that despite everything I just heard, this man is still making my insides weak? Gah, I hate my lack of resolve. Then again, at least anger is taking over now. Moments ago, I was dangerously close to tears and I would have hated that a whole lot more.

"That's not—I didn't mean it like that."

"You sounded pretty convincing with whoever it was on the other line. You have a fixer or something? Someone who talks you through cleaning up these kinds of—" I gesture irately. "Fuck-ups?"

"Alice, please…" He raises his hands up in defense. "Please calm down. I need to tell you something. I was just talking to my brother, Sean, to figure out how to do it."

I snort in frustration. There are so many things I want to say, none of which are calm. But I bite my tongue just long enough for Jack to catch up to me. He stretches his arms out in my direction. A whiff of his cologne frazzles me further, though he still keeps a respectable amount of distance.

To remember the warmth of his arms around me, the softness of his lips against mine, the way his eyes widened with wonder whenever he looked at me throughout our encounter earlier tonight… It's pure agony. And just as I thought things couldn't get any worse, he expresses my greatest fear of the day.

"Tonight wasn't supposed to be a date," he says.

My eyes well up involuntarily. Of course it wasn't. Because why would anyone ask *me* out? Least of all a guy like Jack.

"I gathered that," I whisper. The fact that we ended up in bed was a fuck-up, after all.

"Alice, darling…" He reaches for my face, but I turn away from him and he lowers his hand again. "I asked you to dinner because I needed to tell you the truth. And I wanted to propose something to you. A business deal. Of course, that's off the table now…"

I look up in his direction again. Countless hours I've spent watching him this past week. TV appearances, interviews… And I still can't reconcile that this is the same man. Because the man who stands before me now—though still infuriatingly hot and physically imposing—isn't invincible and immovable. Underneath the cracks in his veneer he's just a guy, who's rambling right now, and trying very hard to backtrack on something that has already transpired. I tried to anticipate a lot of things, but that *he'd* turn out to be the coward in our equation wasn't one of them.

"Alice—"

"Look, it seems like we both had very different ideas of what tonight was meant to be about," I say, in as calm a voice as I can manage.

He nods. "Right, but—"

"Let's act like adults, and—" I try to catch my breath, but my throat is closing up. "If you regret whatever happened, then we can just—"

Hard as I'm trying, I can't contain the frustration

and hurt any longer and I feel myself starting to shake and tremble.

"Alice, no," he whispers. "At least hear me out."

The first tears are starting to flow, and I let them. Silently.

"I don't regret what happened between us," he says.

"No?" I study his face to figure out if he's telling me the truth. Or is he just trying to get me to stop crying, like most guys would?

"I just—Alice, I'm the reason your coffee shop is getting shut down. I wanted to tell you over dinner. I wanted to propose a plan to make things right. I wanted to—"

"A business proposal. Like you just said. Which is now off the table."

"Well, yes. Because I can't—You don't mix—" He takes a deep breath and shrugs.

"Business with sex," I complete the sentence. There's a reason you never hear the term 'business partners with benefits.' Although I'm not even sure friends with benefits should exist either.

Jack looks worse than I feel now. Crushed. Deflated. Defeated. And that's my cue to leave. Open to new opportunities, my ass. He might claim not to regret what happened, but I certainly do. Maybe with the added perspective of hindsight, I will come to appreciate the memory of what happened tonight, when I let my hair down for once.

Right now though, he wasn't the one who fucked up. I was. I got my hopes up and got screwed, in more ways than one. I'm not cut out for this lifestyle. I can't do what some of my friends did before they settled down: enjoy a night of free love without hoping for more…

CHAPTER NINE

* Jack *

I've had so many new experiences tonight, my head is spinning. And despite my best intentions, it all just keeps getting worse. I'm entirely unprepared for how her tears affect me. I'd wanted to help her, not hurt her! This right here is a prime example of why I was right to avoid relationships in the past.

"You don't mix—" I try to find the right words, but they evade me.

"Business with sex," Alice says.

It's like a punch to the gut, hearing her say those words. The coldness in her voice is something I'm unprepared for. She's hurt. Of course she's lashing out in defense. I couldn't have picked worse circumstances to tell her the truth, and now…

Holy hell, she's leaving!

It takes me painfully long to force myself into action and follow her out of the conservatory, through the hallway and across the large open plan living and dining area and up the floating stairs leading to the master bedroom.

She's already at the landing at the top of the steps when I catch her by the arm. She tenses up like a cornered animal underneath my touch, which makes me hate myself even more. I wasn't trying to intimidate her, but that's just the effect I tend to have on people.

"What?" she snaps.

"Is that all this was?" I ask. "Just sex?"

She pauses, then stares at the floor.

"Because if it wasn't, then—" Why is it that this girl has me so screwed up, I can't get a full sentence out? Me! The guy who always knows what to say, no matter who's watching or how many cameras I have shoved in my face.

"Well, that depends," she says.

"On?"

"Was it just business?"

Although her expression has hardened, her eyes are still moist and vulnerable. It takes every ounce of self control not to reach for her again and gather her up in my arms like I'd done earlier. To feel her soft, feminine curves against me once more. The very short time we've spent together so far gave me a taste of something I've never craved before: to matter to someone. To be her rock. Her lifesaver. If only I could turn back time and get another chance to earn that privilege. I'll do anything to make this right again.

"It was, but then on Monday morning, I met

you…" I hear myself say. "And then, everything changed. But the deal was already done; I couldn't just back out at that point."

"Then why the whole business meeting bullshit? Why not just *tell* me when you dropped by—"

"Because I'm a fool, Alice! Because I've spent my entire life in a restaurant kitchen, far away from normal people, who know how to do things like date and talk about feelings and fall in love, and—" I rant.

The corner of her mouth twitches, which tickles the burning dumpster fire that is my heart.

"Married to the business, huh?" she asks.

I press my lips together. Of course she'd remember that.

"Pretty much. Plus, at the time, I assumed you had a boyfriend! The banker."

Alice sighs. "Assumptions truly are the mother of all fuck-ups."

"Will you let me try and make it up to you?" I ask, tentatively reaching for her hands. When she doesn't reciprocate straight away, a fresh surge of nerves washes over me. Until she takes a final step in my direction and wraps her arms around my waist.

"I'm so sorry, Alice. I should have been honest with you."

She tightens her grip on me, and in turn my chest fills with an unfamiliar, reassuring warmth. I just stand there and hold her. This is the real deal. This is what I'd been craving to do all along. To feel her body against mine, leaning on me in a way, is more addictive than anything I've ever experienced.

"I was so focused on finding a solution, to help you get back on your feet, that I—" I stammer.

"I already knew," she says. "I found out about you signing the lease yesterday afternoon."

"And you still—" I lose my train of thought when she buries her face in my chest.

"This is really dumb, but—" she shrugs. "My friends, they picked out my dress, and organized a whole makeover session… They thought I should still turn up, lead you on throughout dinner and then tell you to get stuffed, or something. I don't know what the hell they were thinking."

"Oh?"

She chuckles. "I went along with the dress and the makeover, but I… I just really wanted…"

"Yes?" My voice sounds unusually hoarse.

"I just wanted this. I wanted you."

That's it. Three words to break through my shell and take every last shred of my sanity. I should say something. Anything, to cut through the tension. But I don't have it in me. She wanted me? Why? What did I ever do to deserve her attention, except deceive her and cause her trouble? Things can't really be this simple, can they?

"Everything changed for me too on Monday

morning." Alice leans back and looks up at me. Her eyes are puffy and her lashes are still wet, but she's still the most beautiful woman I've ever seen. It's insane that I'm allowed to be this close to her. "I haven't been able to stop thinking about you since."

Her words are about to make *me* cry now and I don't even care. Is this what life feels like for normal people, for Sean even, since he met Lily? If so, I can understand why he ended up standing on a stage in front of thousands of people—millions, if you count the TV audience—to declare his feelings for her, risking everything including his self respect in the process. I would happily interrupt my next TV appearance to do the same, if only I knew what to bloody say!

"Yeah, same. Much as I wanted to pretend it was the coffee, making me come back again and again—" I mumble.

Her expression twists momentarily and her eyes widen. "You were coming to see *me*?"

I don't know why this is still so damn hard. She needs to hear this. The embarrassing mushy shit, as Sean referred to it. And I need to express it, before my heart explodes out of my chest. "You had me acting like a deranged stalker."

She chuckles softly. "Funny you should say that. I've been stalking you online pretty much nonstop. There's hardly an interview of you on YouTube which I haven't watched by now."

Her confession makes me smile despite myself. All this while I've been so wrapped up in my own guilt, I never considered that she could actually notice me like that too. I'm just not that kind of guy. I'm not the guy who's wanted like this.

"You know that it's all bullshit, right? The whole fame business."

She shrugs. "I did wonder, a few hours into my online research, if you're just playing a role on TV."

I chuckle. "Oh, no. I'm a terrible actor. They don't even script my lines."

"Really?" she asks, her eyes narrowing. "You're literally a different person in reality. Okay, admittedly on Monday morning, you seemed—"

I press my lips together to try and contain another smile. "Grumpy and unlikeable? Don't worry, I've heard worse."

"Grumpy, sure, but still extremely likeable," she corrects me.

I stare down into her beautiful eyes. What have I ever done to deserve her attention? In her shoes, I might have gone along with her friends' crazy revenge plan, but not Alice. She found out that I was the one who had inadvertently upended her life, and… And she still gave me the benefit of the doubt. Who does that, but an angel? Kind and merciful and just everything I am not. It's true what they say; opposites do attract.

"Shall we get back into bed? It's kind of chilly out here." Alice wiggles her eyebrows at me, which makes me chuckle.

"You don't have to tell me twice."

She lets out a surprised squeal when I gather her up in my arms and carry her towards the king-sized bed in the center of the master suite. After depositing her carefully in the middle, I line up a few pillows against the headboard and settle back into them, then pull her into my arms again. She sighs contently, resting her head against my shoulder after I tuck the comforter in around us.

"Tell me something," she starts.

"Yeah?"

"Everything, right from the beginning."

* Alice *

Just like that, we're back in bed. We've been here before, obviously, but not like this. The first time we got under the covers, we were crazed, hormonal, and desperate. There was so much uncertainty hanging in the air, adding to the electricity of the moment.

Now, things are… dare I say comfortable? No, that's not quite right. That sounds boring, whereas things are still electric and exciting.

But the veil of uncertainty has lifted a little, and my usual optimism has been restored. This might just work out, if only…

"Tell me something… Everything, from the beginning," I say.

He tightens his arms around me. That little gesture makes me feel so warm and protected. Like everything is falling into place and we're suddenly on the right track again.

"Okay…" Jack sighs deeply and then starts to talk. With my head resting safely against his shoulder, I find myself enthralled by his deep voice as he tells me the whole story. His plans to open a chain of casual eateries; how Teddington was meant to be the first location of many; how he made a deal with my late boss's son after seeing a couple of other buildings that didn't quite fulfill his needs…

He pauses at our first meeting. Monday morning.

"When I saw you there…" his voice trails off.

I turn slightly and wrap my arm around his waist. God, I love his body. How powerful and strong he feels. I mean, he literally carried me to the bed just now! I feel so small in comparison, especially now when I'm barely able to reach all the way around him from my current position. I've been chubby all my life, so this is a new experience for me. I guess it takes a real man to make me feel all woman and comfortable in my own skin.

"It was like waking up," he explains. "Seeing you, that really short exchange we shared. It was like I'd been sleepwalking my whole life, and I finally opened my eyes."

Just like that, my eyes well up again. That's the most beautiful thing anyone has ever said to me. Crazy. When mostly all I did was tell him good morning. But… I can relate.

"That morning…" The memory has me swooning all over again.

"Yeah?"

"Just as you were leaving, you smiled at me. Only for a split second. I was done for right then," I tell him.

Something in him shifts, just for a moment. Or maybe that's just the butterflies in my own stomach. He tightens his grip on me and chuckles softly. I love that I know what that looks like now. Even though I can't see his face at the moment.

"Smiling in public, on a Monday morning, no less… That doesn't sound anything like me," he remarks.

"Aw, it should be. It can be your new thing."

He shakes his head. "Only with you. For you."

With those words, he shifts the mood yet again. No longer content with the status quo, I push away from him just enough to turn around. The pale green of his eyes looks darker in this light. Almost black. And his lips… Now that we're on the same page, will they taste even sweeter?

I cup his face. The prickle of his beard against my palms puts my entire body on edge. Or maybe it's the hunger in his gaze that does it.

I lean in, as does he. And then, all bets are off. We're not kissing anymore. We're devouring each other. It is sweeter. And spicier. Better in every possible way.

Somehow, I end up straddling him. And just like the first time, he's right there with me. Hard and ready, his energy matches mine perfectly.

"You don't mind I helped myself to your shirt, do you?" I ask, breathlessly, while teasing the top few buttons open to reveal my cleavage.

"Looks a lot better on you than it does on me," he says.

I know he means it, because he's looking at me like a starving man might look at an unlimited buffet. I tug at the next button, and pause on the next. He grabs the shirt, and pulls it open with a swift tug, sending the last couple of buttons flying across the bedroom.

"Your shirt!" I giggle.

"Don't worry, it was worth it," he says.

His hands grab my face, guiding it closer to his. As a result, our bodies close the gap. The heat coming off his bare chest makes my nipples stand so proud, they're getting sore. And I'm wet. So wet.

There's only one way to get relief and my body

knows it. I start grinding down into him. It hits the spot just right.

"Is all this just for me as well?" I ask.

"Always." He grabs my hips, firmly, and keeps me in place, right on top of his hard cock. I love how strong he is, how powerful. I knew it from our very first meeting. Jack *could* dominate me. I never knew how much I needed that. While also trusting that he'd never actually cross the line. He could take whatever he wants, but he would never do it unless I consent.

I wiggle free, and he lets me.

"Show me what you've got, then," I whisper.

He grins at me, while palming his thick shaft, aiming right for me. "Okay, since you asked for it."

Yep. It's all for me. But only if I want it.

He guides me down on top of him until I'm filled up deep. I'm so far gone, I'm reduced to moans and whimpers once we start to move. We don't last long. Neither of us.

With his strong arms around me, I settle down in his warm embrace. It's such a comfort, as well as a stimulant, knowing now that we're both in this together. It doesn't matter that we finished quickly, because we can just do this again. And again. And all over again in the morning.

And that's exactly what we do. And every time I feel him inside of me physically, he takes another little piece of my heart for himself. I vaguely knew it on

Monday, but now I'm certain.

Jack's the one for me. And from everything he's told me, it seems I'm the one for him too.

CHAPTER TEN

*** Alice ***

With a spring in my step, and a perpetual grin on my face, I'm a lot more chipper this morning than my lack of sleep and persistent soreness in my legs and back should have allowed. But there's nothing—absolutely nothing—that can ruin my mood today. The morning after the night that changed everything.

Jack is… He's everything I could dream of and more. Surprisingly sensitive and kind, and an absolute god between the sheets. And like he said, it's all for me. I've won the jackpot and then some. Jack—Jackpot. That's funny.

I just about hear the door chime over the hiss of the espresso machine and turn around with a bright smile on my face. "Amber! Good morning!"

"Morning, Alice."

"I'll get started on that macchiato right away," I turn around, almost dancing to an inaudible tune while setting up everything for her regular order.

"You seem…" Amber mumbles.

"Hmm?" I ask, turning around again.

"I said you seem cheerful."

"Why wouldn't I be?"

"So… last night went okay then?" she asks, frowning so hard her whole forehead scrunches up.

"Oh, yeah. You can say that."

"I'd been wondering, since you never texted me after coming home from your date."

I pause what I'm doing. Shit. I probably should have checked in. She might have been worried, or at the least curious. But, I can't very well whip my phone out in the middle of…all the things Jack and I got up to for most of the night, can I?

"I'm so sorry about that. I hope my silence didn't worry you," I tell her.

"Sooo…" she says again.

I keep quiet while making her drink. She wants details, because of course she does. I'd be curious too in her shoes, but I'm just not sure how much I want to share. It feels too intimate. Too precious. And much too explicit.

"Voila. One vanilla hazelnut macchiato," I tell her, while sliding it across the counter in her direction.

She's all out scrutinizing me now. Head to toe. Can she see the dark circles? I normally don't wear a full face of makeup, but this morning, I had to apply some concealer to get rid of them.

"I don't want to say you owe me more details than that, but…"

"You want more details anyway," I say.

Amber purses her lips. "Well, something! At least until Richard gets here."

I avert my gaze as I feel a knowing smile creep over my face. "Everything went… He was great, you know? We just kind of… connected."

"Connected, right," she remarks. "What about the stuff Lauren told us? Did you guys talk about that at all?"

"Oh, yeah," I make a dismissive gesture. "He told me everything."

"Was this before or after you guys… connected?" Amber asks.

I press my lips together. Does the chronology of everything really matter?

"I mean, our chemistry, it's like—"

"I'm taking that as a 'no.' Honestly, Alice!" she complains. "You can't just trust everyone, you know?"

"I can't really explain how it all went down. It's a bit fuzzy." I try to shrug off the unease that's creeping over me now. Is she right? Or am I just seeing a glimpse of the old, pre-Richard Amber, so suspicious of all men that she found it hard to see the good in him at first too.

"Try, anyway," Amber urges.

"He sent a car to pick me up; I got to the restaurant, and I kind of started flirting with him…

Oh, he'd assumed that Richard was *my* boyfriend, of all things! That's why he was being so cagey at first," I explain.

"You started flirting with him, just as planned, and then? When did the plan change?"

I make a face. "The plan didn't change. I wasn't onboard with the whole revenge idea anyway. It's—" I want to say childish. Immature. But that would derail this conversation instantly. "It's not my style."

"Okay…"

"So, we go back to his place—"

She raises her eyebrows. "Right."

"And we talked things through. And the whole deal was done before we ever met, you know? It's not like he did it on purpose. It was just business."

"Just business, I see," Amber grumbles.

"And he's been trying his best to help me out; with the business plan, even—"

"Even, what?" she pries.

She has a way of getting what she wants, from whoever. I just never realized how well it works on me too.

"He was going to propose a business deal, actually, before we ended up—"

"Oh?" Her eyes widen. "What was the deal?"

I exhale sharply. Oh dear. I've said too much.

"What was it?" she repeats.

"It's not really relevant now, because you can't mix

business, and—"

"Okay." Amber sighs and shakes her head. "I know I'm being a hard ass, but I'd hate to see you get hurt."

"You care, I know," I whisper.

She finally picks up her drink and smiles briefly at me before heading to her seat.

God. I hate that she made me tell her all that. I wasn't ready. I'd been floating on cloud nine since I woke up, and now… Now, I don't know what I am anymore. Because the uncertainty that hung over our heads last night hasn't actually gone at all. I let myself get distracted by my feelings for Jack, and now…

The door chime goes off again, and for a moment, I hope it's him.

"Morning, Alice!" Richard grins widely at me. "Had to make a detour this morning." He holds up a couple of brand new notepads. "Writerly supplies."

"Good morning." I force a smile, trying not to show my disappointment. "I'll have your coffee ready for you in just a minute."

"Take your time, Alice. I'll be here all day." Richard chuckles softly on the way to their regular table, where Amber is already typing furiously on her laptop. Watching him greet her with a warm embrace from behind and gentle kiss to the temple makes me feel a little sick.

Why did Amber have to rain on my parade like

that? After months of silent yearning, this morning I finally thought I'd found that for myself. A genuinely good man, who likes me for me. No hidden agendas or motives. Just love? And now… Ugh!

* Jack *

I'm distracted all morning and catch myself staring off into the distance more than once as visions of last night and this morning flood my memory again and again. Sweet Alice… She's taken over my every thought, making it impossible for me to do or think of much else. But there's still something else; a nagging undercurrent of restlessness, which I can't seem to shake.

"You haven't even touched your coffee," Carrie comments, when she enters my office carrying a stack of paperwork.

Her sudden appearance makes me flinch, which is even more unlike me than the staring and brooding. She's right and she's getting suspicious.

"Carrie, be a dear and set up another meeting with the lawyers today," I tell her.

She sets down the papers and looks me up and down once. "You already have a meeting with the architect at eleven. It's been on your calendar for a week now, and I've even got the preliminary design brief right here." She brushes her index finger across the paperwork she just set down to make her point.

I sigh in frustration. Architect. Ugh. I can't even focus long enough to remember to drink my morning cup of coffee before it goes cold; how am I going to discuss the plans for the upcoming restaurant with him under these circumstances? I'm bound to mess things up at this rate, and I can't have that. Plus, I can't shake the feeling that something is very wrong. What, though? Surely, everything went great with Alice once I told her the truth, which leaves just one possible answer: my intuition is telling me something is wrong on the business end of things.

"No can do, Carrie. I need to see the lawyers first."

"Okay… so I'll reschedule him, then. Any idea when you might be available?"

I make a face and shake my head.

"Is there a problem I should know about?" she pries.

I shake my head again. "I'm… I'm just not fully clear on my vision for the place yet."

"This doesn't happen to be about that girl, does it?" she asks.

I shoot a disapproving glance her way. Perceptive as ever. I hate it. How did she even find out about Alice? Does she have me under surveillance or something?

"That's really not—"

"I've been with you for how many years now?

Eight?" she asks. "It's my job to pick up on things. To always stay one step ahead of everything that's going on in your business."

"In the *business*, sure," I say.

"You had me print out that partnership contract, remember? So, I did some digging," she counters.

Sure, I guess that part was business, I just hadn't expected her to *read* the contract while printing it out, never mind doing some 'digging,' whatever that means. I scowl at her, which seems to have no effect at all. "I don't see how that's any of your—"

"Oh, but it is. Because my job is secure only as long as this ship sails smoothly. And if it doesn't, then it's my responsibility to get things back on the right track. Excuse me for mixing my metaphors, but you get the message."

"Carrie, I need you to set up that meeting as soon as possible. Precisely to get things back on track, as you say. And if it makes you feel any better, the partnership contract is off the table anyway." Well, at least in its current form, it is.

She presses her lips together tightly and maintains her almost impenetrable poker face. But she's pleased. I can see it. And somehow, that doesn't reassure me at all.

"Okay, I'll make the necessary calls. Is there anything else you need me to do? Maybe a fresh cup of coffee?" She picks up the tray and hovers near my desk, waiting for my reply.

"No thanks, that'll be all for now." I watch as she leaves my office, closing the door behind herself. I need to get my head straightened out, stat. This state of mind right here is how mistakes are made.

Alice, Alice, Alice… What have you done to me? My fingers hover over the darkened screen of my phone. Well maybe, if I check in with her real quick, I'll be able to get her out of my mind for a little while before I fall apart.

It rings twice, thrice. A feeling of relief washes over me when the call finally connects.

"Good morning, Alice!"

"Jack," she answers. "Hi."

I frown. Not quite the enthusiasm I was hoping for.

"Ever since you left this morning—" I start.

"Yeah…"

"I haven't been able to stop thinking about you." Right. That felt awkward.

"Me neither," she says.

Well, that's promising at least? But then, why does she sound so unlike her usual self? Where's the friendly chatter? The cheerful warmth? Where's *my* Alice?

"Is everything alright?" I ask.

She sighs. "Yeah… It's just… I think I'm suffering from a bit of sleep deprivation." I nod along while she talks. Sure. That would make sense. Except, in her own words, she'd been staying up late googling me ever since our first meeting, so she would have been functioning on less sleep for a week now. What changed now? Is she having second thoughts about what happened between us?

"Tell you what, I'm free all morning," I lie. "Let's meet up and talk. I'll come to you; what do you say?"

"Okay." She sighs again, or is she stifling a yawn? Maybe the poor girl is just tired like she says. After everything we got up to all night, that may just be the most logical explanation. I might have just accepted that, if it wasn't for the growing sense of unease in my belly. I'm nervous, of all things. What the hell have I got to be nervous about? Everything's good between us, isn't it?

"I'll be there in twenty minutes, Alice," I tell her, while pushing my chair back and grabbing my phone.

CHAPTER ELEVEN

*** Alice ***

Jack is coming. Here. Now. And I'm…

I glance over at Amber and Richard, who are absorbed in their own little bubble of work and affectionate banter. The door chime startles me, and I force myself into action to serve the new customers. It's a busy morning, because of course it is. It's always busy first thing in the morning. And Jack is coming over. Twenty minutes, he said.

And I'll be busy making drinks and won't be able to talk to him, really. And what would I even say? And Amber will be watching, potentially listening in. I won't be able to duck out and talk to Jack in private.

I should have told him not to bother. That we'll talk after hours, in peace. But no. That would have been sensible and smart, whereas I feel stupid and out of control right now.

It takes me a little longer than normal to finish the current drinks order, and then another. And another. I try to mumble my usual pleasantries as I hand the customers their drinks. It all feels fake. For the first time in years, I'm not enjoying my work. I don't even know if I'll still be doing this in three months, once Jack takes over the lease.

I nearly burn my hand on the milk steamer and take a moment to gather myself. I can't even make a cappuccino properly right now. How am I expecting to put together a business plan, and present it at the bank? And Jack was supposed to help me, but he said his mystery proposal is off the table now, and I don't even know what he was thinking before we ended up in bed together. God, I'm so stupid. I've done this whole thing ass-backwards. No wonder Amber was frustrated with me! I'm even more frustrated with myself right now.

The door chime goes off again.

"Just a minute!" I call over my shoulder, while finishing the last pending order.

I turn around, tray in hand, and spot him. And my knees go weak.

He's even more handsome this morning than I remember from last night. And I remember… a lot, in vivid detail. On top of me, underneath me, with his lips on mine, his arms cradling my shoulders…

"Alice," he says. "Good morning."

His voice is a low rumble, and the way he looks at me sends shivers down my spine. I wish I could adequately express how seeing him here, in my world, fills me with warmth and chaos all at once. I wish I could have just enjoyed the moment, but my earlier exchange with Amber has made me question everything. I shoot a quick glance behind Jack, where Amber is curiously eyeing the both of us already.

"Morning, Jack!" I manage to reply, trying to sound casual while my heart races. I set the tray down and wipe my hands on my apron, nervously fidgeting with the fabric. "You really didn't need to come."

"I thought we should talk." His expression tenses, and my heart races even faster. Has any variation of the phrase 'we need to talk' ever led to a perfectly pleasant conversation? I'm not sure.

"Okay," I say cautiously. "But it's quite busy right now." Just as I finish my sentence, the door chime goes off and several of my regular morning customers enter together.

He follows my gaze and his stance softens again. "Right. Work comes first. I can lend a hand, if that helps."

"Are you serious?" I blink, surprised. "You want to… serve coffee?"

"I'm more than capable of working an espresso machine, you know," he says with a playful smirk.

I'm speechless, only letting out a surprised chuckle as he makes his way around the counter and takes his position beside me. As I mindlessly hand him Deedee's apron, my eyes meet Amber's, who is still staring at the two of us with her hand covering her mouth.

"We'll get these orders out in no time. Together," Jack says.

My heart flutters and my chest swells with… What the hell even is this sensation? Pride? Even in my wildest dreams I couldn't have predicted finding myself here this morning, with Jack-effing-Cleary working alongside me.

"Alright, but just until things settle down," I mumble.

"Deal," he replies, while shooting one of his very rare smiles in my direction. This man… He's an enigma. Just when I try to get a handle on him, he does something so completely out of the ordinary that I still have no idea where we stand.

The morning rush pushes on, and for the better part of forty minutes we take turns interacting with customers and preparing drinks. He starts off a little wooden and overly serious, but soon starts getting the hang of things, even exchanging pleasantries with some of the customers while wrapping up their takeaway orders. And his presence isn't just throwing *me* off balance, it's having an effect on my clientele as well, with some sneaking pictures of him on their phones while he goes about the work.

It's not every day that you see a celebrity chef behind the counter of your local coffee shop. I'm surprised no one has asked for an autograph yet.

Eventually though, the crowd begins to thin. Once I'm finally done with the last order, I wipe my forehead and look up to find him standing a few steps away from me, arms crossed, observing me with a subtle smile playing on his lips.

"How'd I do, boss?" he asks, his eyes sparkling with mischief.

I can't help myself and rush over in his direction, throwing my arms around his shoulders to give him a quick hug. "You totally rescued me, that's how you did. And the coffee wasn't half bad either. Though, most of the customers were so shocked, they probably wouldn't notice any different even if you'd served them cups of dishwater instead."

He rests his hands on my hips and gazes deeply into my eyes. "I'm glad to hear it. Because that's what I want, more than anything."

"What's that? Being a good barista?" I joke.

"Rescuing you."

Just like that, he takes my breath away again. With those two little words, as well as the intensity in his eyes. Does he mean that, really?

He clears his throat before clarifying. "That's what I wanted to talk to you about."

"Oh?" I ask. I'm glad he's still holding onto me, because otherwise, I might find my knees trembling underneath me. It's crazy how much of an effect his sheer presence has on me. Or maybe that's just because of the muscle ache our antics from last night inspired.

"Okay," I begin, nervously scanning the room for an empty table. "Shall we take a seat?"

"Actually, no. It was naive of me to barge in here expecting to have this big, serious conversation when you have a business to run," he says. "We'll talk, but over dinner. For the moment, I just want to say one thing."

"Yes?" My voice sounds weak, uncertain. I hate it. This isn't how I want to present myself, least of all with him. But somehow, I can't help myself. I feel like I've just gotten off the wildest roller coaster ride of my life and I'm still shaken by it.

"You're not going to close down the coffee shop once my lease starts."

"I'm not?" I ask.

"No. It's going to stay open. And it's going to be exactly how it is now, with you in charge."

"It is?" I parrot, completely confused by what he's trying to tell me. "But it's your lease. For your restaurant."

"I'm not going to open a restaurant here anymore."

I shake my head, utterly confused by what he's trying to tell me. "I don't get it."

"We'll work out the details later, but Alice." He takes a deep breath and cups my face in his hands.

"Sweet, wonderful Alice…"

I blink up at him and wait for everything to make sense.

"I want this for you. Your dream come true. Let me help make it a reality. In any case, I think I just demonstrated that I do know a little bit about what it takes to make a decent cup of coffee," he jokes, which makes my heart skip a beat, but then, his expression turns serious again. "So, it's only natural for me to back this venture. To back you. Whatever you need, I'm here. This space, it's going to remain yours. And if it's funding you need, I can sort that out too."

"What if…" I wonder aloud.

"Anything," he confirms.

"What if I don't want anything… Just you?" I ask.

His eyes soften, along with the rest of his presence. A soft tremor travels through his shoulders as he takes a deep breath. "That… you already have. For as long as you want."

* Jack *

This was hard. Harder perhaps than any other conversation I've ever had. And yet, it was also effortless, because this is Alice I'm talking to. And she makes me feel on top of the world with every smile she sends my way. I couldn't have done this with anyone else.

"What if I don't want anything?" she asks. It's a question that could send me into a spiral of self doubt, if not for what she follows it up with. "Just you."

This is the moment when I know. This is it. She's the one. And despite Carrie's warnings earlier, and the fact that I still haven't talked this over with my legal team, I am more certain than ever that I'm doing the right thing. This woman is my alpha and my omega. I would move mountains for her; what's a little funding and a building lease?

"That… you already have, for as long as you want," I mumble.

Our eyes are locked onto each other, and despite the bustling café around us, it feels like we're the only two people in the world. The intensity of the moment is overwhelming, and I can see the reflection of my own emotions in her eyes—a mix of excitement, fear, and hope.

"Jack, I…" Alice starts, but her voice trails off as she searches for the right words. She takes a deep breath, and I can see the gears turning in her head as she tries to process what I've just said.

"I know it's a lot to take in," I say softly, trying to reassure her. "But I mean every word. I want to be here for you, Alice. In any way you'll have me."

She bites her lip, a habit I've come to adore, and looks down at our intertwined hands. "I just… I never expected this. Any of this. I don't know what to say."

"You don't have to say anything right now," I tell her, lifting her chin gently with my fingers so that she meets my gaze again. "Just know that I want to be there for you. We can figure everything else out over dinner tonight. If you're free, that is."

Her eyes well up with tears, but she blinks them back, a determined look replacing the uncertainty from before. "Okay," she says, her voice steady and resolved. "Okay, we'll figure it out. Together."

A smile spreads across my face, and I can't help but lean in and press a soft kiss to her lips. It's a promise, a seal of our newfound partnership—both in business and in life. When we pull away, her cheeks are flushed, and her eyes are shining with happiness.

"Together," I echo, my heart swelling with a warmth I haven't felt ever before. This is right. This is how it's supposed to be. I may not be much of a Prince Charming, but at least I can fix the mess I caused her. Coffee to the Rescue will stay open, no matter what happens next.

Just then, I spot a young woman with long dark blonde hair observing us very keenly from across the counter.

"Amber," Alice greets her. "Meet Jack. Jack, meet my friend Amber. She's the one I told you about."

I wrack my brain for whatever Alice might have

told me last night. Is she the friend who's dating the banker, or the one who cooked up that whole revenge scheme?

"Um, sorry to interrupt whatever's going on between you two," Amber says, looking sheepish. "But you guys are about one customer away from having your pictures go viral. People are calling their friends, who are calling their friends. We're about to be overrun."

She gestures at the entrance, where a small group of women has assembled, curiously peeping through the glass door and chatting excitedly between each other.

"Ah. Yeah," I grumble. Seems I'm demonstrating yet again that I'm only just starting to learn the lessons my little brother Sean has already had to learn the hard way. People in the public eye can't just do what normal folk take for granted.

"Oh, crap." Alice lets go of me and brushes her hand past her forehead while staring at the small crowd outside.

"I think…" I start taking my apron off.

"We should talk about this later. Over dinner, like you said," Alice completes my thought.

"I think that's an excellent idea," Amber says.

CHAPTER TWELVE

*** Alice ***

The drive to Jack's house feels like an eternity, even though it's only about half an hour from the café by chauffeur driven car. My heart races with anticipation, remembering all the sweet promises he made this morning. When we finally pull up to his driveway, I pause to gather my nerves, giving the driver just enough time to open the door for me.

"Here we are," he says.

I force a smile and a nod. "Thanks."

Jack's already waiting in the open doorway when I get up the steps.

"Alice, I'm so glad to see you," he says, his voice a low rumble that sends shivers down my spine. He takes my hand and ushers me inside, closing the door behind us. From the corner of my eye, I spot a glimmer of a smile, one of those rare ones he seems to reserve just for me, and I feel more at home. Why am I even nervous right now? From everything Jack told me earlier today, it's pretty clear that we're on the same page. He's literally giving me my own coffee shop, from the sounds of things. So why do I still feel like I'm about to wake up from this perfect dream? Why do I still seem to doubt what's right in front of me?

The house is filled with a delicious aroma, which instantly makes my stomach growl. Despite my best efforts to check out my surroundings this time, I have only eyes for him, leading the way into the kitchen.

"The food smells amazing," I say.

"I hope you like it," he replies, lifting the lid off a pot to stir its contents. "It's a recipe I've been perfecting for a while."

He catches me staring and turns off the gas before walking over to me. He pauses briefly before resting his hands on my upper arms. Is he nervous too? If so, he's hardly letting me see it. Meanwhile, my heart is frantically trying to jump out of my chest right now. More so now that I can feel the warmth of his skin through my sweater.

"There's so much I want to say," he murmurs, his eyes locked onto mine. "And now…"

"Me too," I whisper, enjoying the rush of sensations as a familiar feeling of safety fills my entire being. I'm okay. As long as he's holding me like this, everything is always going to be okay, isn't it?

"I'm rather new to all this, but I hope you'll bear with me."

I press my lips together tightly, trying not to grin,

because he's so adorable right now. My own nerves take a backseat now that I've detected his. Here he is, Jack-effing-Cleary, a powerhouse in the kitchen, and easily the sternest cooking show judge on television, with a sheepish glint in his eye, fumbling over his words.

"What?" he asks, mirroring my smile. Just like that, I'm breathless again.

"Jack," I start, suddenly forgetting the rest of my sentence as I'm swept up in his stare.

"Alice." I love how he says my name. It makes me giddy and calms me down all at once. "I meant every word I said to you earlier."

This can't be happening. I'm not Cinderella, or any of the other fairytale princesses facing their prince, and yet… He's sweeping me off my feet with just one look. And one word: my name.

"I should have done this sooner; yesterday, even. Hell, I should have done it pretty much the moment we met, but I was too dumb to recognize my own feelings…" he fumbles on.

He's nothing if not persistent, trying again and again to get his point across. God, I love that about him. I love pretty much everything about him…

"I want you to know that my offer stands, no matter what. Whether this thing between us works out or not, we'll figure it out. I won't leave you hanging or impose any conditions on you, ever. I want to see you succeed, Alice. I want you to achieve your dreams. That's what part of me has wanted right from the beginning."

"What about the other part," I wonder aloud, barely audible over the thumping of my heart.

The corner of his mouth twitches knowingly. "The other part came out to play last night."

"I've got that part too," I tell him.

"Yeah?"

"Oh, it's making it hard to focus on anything else." I stare at him, and he stares at me and nothing seems to matter anymore. Exactly like last night. Which is what got us in all this trouble in the first place.

He inhales sharply. For a moment, the rose tinted glasses seem to lift off his eyes and he focuses on me with a seriousness I haven't seen in a while. This is business-Jack, I decide. The change in him would be unnerving, if I wasn't also so mesmerized by the emotional depth I continue to see in his eyes.

"I'm serious, Alice. I'm really quite inept at relationships. Never had much time for them. But ever since I've met you, I wished I'd put in the work, just so I'd know how to handle this."

"We can figure it all out together," I say.

"I didn't have a happy childhood, didn't get much in the way of support at home. I got out at seventeen, interning at some country retreat way up north and I never looked back. Until fairly recently, I wasn't even on speaking terms with Sean. Not since our parents passed, anyway. That's thirty years of my life spent working. Alone."

"I'm sorry," I whisper.

He shakes his head, his expression solemn. "Don't be. It's been a pretty good life so far. The thing is, I never learned how to do… this."

I feel like crying. Like stopping him and telling him I don't need anything special. I just want his arms around me, and my lips against his, and everything will be alright. But words evade me once more.

"I've spent my entire life convincing myself that I wasn't cut out for love. Never gave it much of a second thought. Until you, Alice." While he talks, my brain is working overtime, analyzing, piecing things together. "And now… I realize how unfair that is to you. You deserve the very best. You deserve to have *all* your dreams come true, both personal as well as professional. And I'll do everything in my power to make that happen. I'll make sure your future is secured, no matter what happens between us on a personal level. Because I've already proven that I'll ruin this sooner or later."

Just as he finishes talking, I find myself shaking my head. I've achieved clarity. It all makes sense now. "No."

"No?"

"Teething problems," I tell him. "Nothing's going

to get ruined unless we decide to stop trying to make it work. You're being too hard on yourself."

He averts his gaze from me and takes my hand. "You're too good for me, Alice. Too sweet and forgiving."

Now that I see what he's doing, I'm not letting myself get swept up in sentimentality. Not yet, anyway. Because there are still things that need to be said. Things that *I* need to express, which don't fit into the narrative he's trying to spin. "Maybe I'm just the right amount of sweet, and you're just the right amount of salty," I counter.

He chuckles softly. "We even each other out? Is that what you're saying?"

"A perfect dish needs just the right balance of both, doesn't it?" I ask. I'm pretty sure I heard him say that during one of those interviews I watched of him.

He looks into my eyes again, and I can see my progress. I'm piercing through those walls of his, digging my way down towards that part he was hinting at earlier. The one that came out to play last night.

"Our pasts don't define our future," I tell him. "You tell me I deserve the best, but from my point of view? Men haven't exactly been queuing around the block to ask me out. Over the course of this year, every single one of my friends has fallen in love and with it, out of my life, and I've stood on the sidelines, watching. I've been happy for them of course, but it's been hard not to feel jealous. Somehow, I'd ended up on the same path as you. I was too busy with the coffee shop to make an effort to actually get out there and pursue a relationship. Until you walked in that morning. You're it, Jack. You're the one I want. And it's doing neither of us any favors to pretend otherwise."

As I'm speaking, his expression falls and falls. Gone is the little smile that had just been tugging at the corner of his mouth, as well as the crinkly lines on either side of his eyes. The sparkle in his eyes fades as they widen, staring at me almost in disbelief. For a moment, I'm gripped by fear. That I've said the wrong thing, maybe jumped to conclusions, or hurt his feelings somehow. He's probably never had anyone talk to him the way I am. Jack is used to being the one to tell it how it is, and I'm pushing back. I just stare back in silence, worrying whether to start apologizing or doubling down.

But then, he reaches for my cheek. His hand rests there for a moment, nearly burning a hole into my skin, it's so intense. And for a split second, I wonder if that's a tear in the corner of his eye.

"I wasn't ready to hear that," he confesses. "I guess, I never expected to."

I press my lips together as tightly as I can. Because

if I don't, I might just scream, I'm so tense.

"But… I feel the same way. You're the one for me too, Alice." His voice is so low and gravelly now, it makes all the hair on the back of my neck stand up. In the best possible way. And the tenderness in his gaze just completes the picture. This is pure fairytale material. I thought everyone else's love stories were super romantic, but my own… It's reaching new levels of gooeyness. I guess Jack really is intent on making every single one of my dreams come true.

I exhale sharply, chuckling softly as my eyes well up. "Oof! That's a relief."

"I couldn't have said it quite that eloquently though… Hence the meal I prepared for you. I figured, that's something I'm unlikely to mess up. If you're hungry tonight, that is." The way he looks at me, with a mixture of trepidation and care, leaves no room for refusal.

"Starving," I say.

"Glad to hear it. Because I really would love the chance to feed you," he says, before clearing his throat and adding in a half-whisper: "Every night for the rest of our lives if you'll have me."

I swallow hard. Every night? Rest of our lives? I know that's what his earlier confession hinted at, but part of me still thinks I'm dreaming.

He leads me to the dining table, which is already set with candles and wine. I feel like I'm floating rather than walking into my own happy ending. It's nice to be on the receiving end of someone else's care for once. Could I get used to this?

We sit down, and he serves the food—a seemingly simple risotto with wild mushrooms and parmesan that somehow out beats every single other risotto I've ever eaten. As we take our first bites, the mood lightens a little. The conversation flows more easily between us as we chat about this and that. Lighter topics as first, then moving onto deeper questions interspersed with smiles and laughter. After the tense build-up to the conversation we've already shared, I can finally relax. We exchange stories of our pasts, distant as well as recent, over the second serving of risotto.

My favorite thing? How he seems to enjoy his meal too. He loves what he does, just as I enjoy my work at the coffee shop. No wonder he is where he is; his drive and ambition are forces of nature.

After dinner, Jack takes my hand and leads me to the living room. We settle onto the couch, our bodies pressed close together. He puts his arm around me, and I lean into him, feeling content and safe, but also… unsettled and starving for something else.

"You know," he says softly, "I've been thinking about you all day. About last night, about this morning, about everything in between."

I swallow hard, words evading me once more.

Because this was always coming. After the confessions and the food and the heart-to-heart, I have been anticipating… dessert. The same one I also haven't been able to stop thinking about.

CHAPTER THIRTEEN

*** Jack ***

"I've been thinking about you all day. About last night, about this morning, about everything in between," I say.

"Me too," Alice whispers, after a short pause.

We've been here before, with our arms around each other, and yet... It's different and new. Maybe because I've finally spoken my truth. All of it, without omissions. And she's still here. For me, and also for herself, which is even more meaningful. To know that she wants this as much as I do means everything to me. The heaviness I'd been carrying around with me all week is finally gone without a trace. In its place, there are new challenges, doubts, what-ifs.

"You don't care about our differences?" I ask, my eyes probing hers for any hint of trepidation, but finding none.

"That you're salty?" she teases sweetly, making me smile despite myself.

"That. And that I must be about two decades older than you," I clarify.

She shakes her head, but doesn't take her eyes off me even for a second. I'm used to being watched, but right now, I feel *seen*. "You're like a fine wine. I think you're better this way," she says.

I want to correct her, and tell her that actually, wine doesn't get any better after a certain age, at some point it just gets old. But I don't. Because it's the intention behind her words that matters. Sean was right. She *is* making me more agreeable. And patient. And so much more.

"And that I've never been much of a romantic, so you'll have to teach me a few new tricks maybe."

She bites her bottom lip, pretending to think it over, but the amused glint in her eye gives her away. "You proved yourself to be an excellent learner back at the coffee shop, so I'm not foreseeing any problems there."

I grin and avert my gaze. It tickles me how she talks to me. Because nobody else would dare. She's always been different, I knew it from the first moment we met. She challenged me even then, in the subtlest way possible. I love how much more overt she has become.

Unable to act cool any longer, I reach over and cup her face in my hands. How small and fragile she looks all of a sudden, with her big brown eyes staring right into my soul. Such beauty… All for me?

"You're perfect, Alice. You know that?"

"No, but you are," she breathes.

I silence her with my lips, tasting her mouth for the first time tonight. I forget why I resisted for so long. I guess I thought if we started doing this, I'd never gather the courage to say everything I needed to.

Her tongue meets mine just like all those previous times we kissed. But it's also different now. Softer. More deliberate. Gentle enough to bring tears to my eyes. She tastes even sweeter than the last time.

"I love you, Jack," she seems to say.

I must be imagining that, because it doesn't sound right. It's just not the sort of thing I've ever heard.

"Alice," I groan, when her hands feel their way around my chest. She did this last night also, caressing me. And it drove me wild then too. Exactly because I'm not used to it. Every time my body gets a hint of affection from her, it screams for more.

"I love you," she repeats, in between further kisses.

This time there's no denying it. I pull away and look at her. Eyes at half-mast, flushed cheeks and red lips made for kissing. She's a vision to behold. My heart is racing out of control, and my brow is getting sweaty. Just when I thought I got the hang of things, she does something completely out of syllabus.

"I…" I mumble.

"I get it," she says. "It's too soon."

I shake my head, because… it's not. It's not too

soon. I just feel incredibly stupid that I didn't think to use those words earlier. Because they perfectly describe the storm of emotions that's been unfurling inside my chest.

"I love you too."

Her eyebrows pull together in surprise. As though she's as shocked as I was to hear those words directed at her. That's when I realize the gravity of everything she's been trying to tell me over dinner. Her fears and insecurities about being the only one of her friends left single. How lonely she must have felt, working by herself in that shop every single day like she said. Still, she stayed cheerful and in good spirits, no doubt brightening up many a customer's mornings, just like she did mine on Monday.

She noticed me, just as I noticed her. Crazy. I can't imagine how nervous she would have felt after I asked her to dinner yesterday. How conflicted, once she found out I'd signed the lease. All this while I was so wrapped up in my own doubts and worries, and didn't spend nearly enough time considering hers.

But I see her now. I see her selflessness and love for everyone else. Her reluctance, when I offered to pitch in earlier at the shop. She's used to doing everything on her own, without asking for help unless absolutely necessary. That's why she looked so pained when she requested me to look at her business plan a few days ago.

It all makes sense now that I'm taking a step back. These are the things that spoke to me since our first meeting. All the little cues I never noticed before, perfectly aligned to awaken my dormant heart.

She didn't knowingly do it, but something in her called out to me for help. And I want nothing more than to answer. That's why I've felt so guilty all week. I wasn't listening to my instincts then. But now I am, and I know what I have to do.

It doesn't matter that I've spent my entire life being a grumpy prick who never had time for anyone else, as long as I make time for *her*. That's what she was trying to tell me earlier. We just have to keep putting in the work for *us*. And as a born workaholic, work's easy. Doubly so when it's for her or us, rather than just for me.

She's still staring at me, speechless, which makes me smile. I've been doing that so much lately, my cheeks are getting weirdly sore.

"Alice," I tell her, pausing for maximum effect. "I love you."

Her eyes well up and she wraps her arms around my neck, pulling herself into me tightly. It's a beautiful feeling. Finally, I did it. I said the right thing; I opened myself to her fully. And now my chest feels a whole lot lighter as a result.

I gather her up in my arms, positioning her sideways on the sofa with her head on the armrest, before raising my head just far back enough to be able to kiss her again. She answers me hungrily, caressing, squeezing, feeling me through my shirt. I was hard already, obviously. That's the effect she's been having on me physically. But I'm also determined not to repeat last night's performance.

Lovely as it was, acting out all our urges and desires in a rush, tonight calls for something more special. Tonight's going to be all about her. To pamper her like the queen she is.

Her hand, reaching down my side, onto my hip and squeezing in between us to feel my erection almost derails me. But not quite.

"Not yet," I tell her, while peeling her shirt up and over her stomach and chest. She gasps when I make my way down, kissing her cleavage and gently nipping at the soft skin on her stomach.

I trace a path with my lips down her navel, my hands exploring the luxurious curves of her body, committing every inch of her to memory. Her breath hitches as I reach the waistband of her jeans, and I look up to meet her gaze, seeking silent permission, which she gives me with a silent stare and a bite on her bottom lip.

With deliberate slowness, I unbutton and unzip her, my fingers brushing against the sensitive skin beneath. I can feel her tremble slightly under my touch, and it spurs me on. I slide her jeans down, revealing the lace beneath, a tantalizing contrast to her no-nonsense outfit for the night. None of it detracts from her beauty. She could be wearing a paper bag and still be the most gorgeous creature walking this world.

I hook my fingers under the elastic, pulling it down gently, exposing her fully to me. Her scent is intoxicating, a mix of sweetness and arousal that makes my head spin. I pause for a moment, just taking her in, the sight of her up close almost too much to bear.

My right hand is itching to give myself some relief, but I refrain. I'll not be selfish this time. *Focus on her; she deserves it.*

My tongue darts out, sampling her for the first time. She's soft and warm, and she tastes like heaven. I hear her moan softly as I explore her with my mouth, each sound she makes fueling my desire. I'm careful, gentle, wanting to draw this out, to make her feel cherished and worshipped.

I find her most sensitive spot, circling it with the tip of my tongue, before closing my lips around it and sucking gently. She arches into me, her fingers threading through my hair, urging me on. I increase the pressure, matching the rhythm of her hips as they begin to move in sync with my affections.

Her breathing becomes erratic, her moans more insistent. Every time she utters my name, I'm filled to the brim with sensations I hardly know how to deal with. So, I channel them down here, from my mouth into her core. I can feel her thighs tensing, her body coiling like a spring. I know she's close, and I want nothing more than to send her over the edge, to give her the release she so desperately needs. Which we both need.

"Let me feel you," I whisper into her sweet pussy. "Let me hear you scream."

I slide a finger inside her, then another, curling them in a beckoning motion, and her response is almost immediate. She cries out my name, her body trembling as waves of pleasure crash over her. I continue to suckle her clit, drawing out her orgasm until she's limp and sated beneath me.

All the while, my cock is rock hard and fighting desperately to break free from the confines of my pants. I know I could join her in her release, with nothing more than a buck of my hips, grinding against whatever comes in my way. But I don't want to take my focus off her yet.

As her breathing slows and her grip on my hair loosens, I kiss my way back up her body. The contentment written on her face fills me with a sense of pride unlike anything I've ever felt before. None of the achievements of my 47 years on this earth so far could prepare me for this. I've truly arrived in her arms.

"You are exquisite," I whisper, while planting soft kisses on the side of her neck.

She stirs, her hands slipping in underneath my shirt and roaming my sides and back. "Make love to me. I need to feel you too," she demands.

It's as if she knows I can't deny her anything. Especially not something my body has been screaming out for from the moment she walked into my house tonight. We make short work of my belt and trousers. While I discard my clothes on the floor, she wiggles out of the remainder of hers too. Her moist lips still parted with urgent breaths, she's a vision of perfection. And also all the inspiration I need to fulfill her every demand.

I get up on all fours, and position myself between her lusciously full thighs. She's dripping with her own arousal, and remnants of my saliva; I slip right in there and I'm home. Is it always going to be like this? I'd like to think so. As good or even better, as we master each other's favorite moves. Because we might be facing a busy few months. With the expansion of her coffee shop—after all, the lease on the adjoining art gallery is already signed too—and the regular demands of my restaurant business and TV appearances… But we'll always make time for this.

It took a while for me to realize. Living for yourself is fine and well, but it's empty and meaningless compared to what we share. From now on, neither of us will be married to the business.

On the contrary, perhaps we'll—That's a thought for another time.

Slowly, gently, our bodies move in perfect harmony. Me on top as she requested, I'm at a perfect vantage point to admire every hurried breath and micro expression my efforts earn me. The most beautiful woman on earth—I'll spend every free moment of my days to remind her of that. I'll learn what I need to. I'll be all I can be. She's the only one who ever made me feel this way, the only one who ever saw me like this.

It's all for her. Always has been, always will be.

With every touch, every kiss, every whispered affection and every thrust of my hips, we get one step closer to becoming one. Now, and for the rest of our lives.

EPILOGUE

* Alice *

Four Months Later.

The grand opening of the new and improved Coffee to the Rescue is finally happening, and I can hardly contain my excitement. The past few months have been a whirlwind of planning, renovating, and bucket loads of hard work. Today is the day it all comes to fruition.

I'm standing off to the side, leaning against the pastel pink mantel of the fireplace that was always my favorite part of the old shop, while looking out at the bustling crowd.

The café has been transformed. With Jack's help and investment, we've expanded into the space next door, knocking down walls and creating an open, airy atmosphere. The once small and cozy coffee shop is now a spacious, inviting haven, filled with the aroma of fresh coffee and pastries, and thanks to Jack's guidance and influence, a limited selection of freshly prepared small plates and warm snacks.

And best of all, it hasn't lost its character and charm. It still feels like home to me, and I wake up every day excited to come here, while also maintaining more of a work-life balance, thanks to

Jack's help with the management side of the business.

Jack is here, but he's doing his best to stay out of the spotlight. He's been an absolute rock throughout this process, offering support, advice, and endless encouragement.

I catch his eye from across the room, and he smiles at me, a warm, reassuring smile that makes my heart flutter. What a difference there is between the first time I laid eyes on him just about five months prior and now. Gone is that perpetual crease in between his eyebrows, which used to betray just how seriously he took himself and life in general. He's even starting to develop some laughter lines in the corner of his eyes, which I can't stop admiring. He really is like a fine wine, or as he pointed out, more like an expensive cognac: better with age.

The door chimes, and I look up to see a young couple entering. Jack greets the solidly built man who doesn't look much older than me with a pat on the back, and his petite blonde companion with a smile and a nod. That's about as affectionate as Jack gets with anyone other than me, so these two must be special. He leads them over to me.

"Alice, this is Ethan, you might have seen him on his own show on the Home TV network, and his lovely girlfriend, Sarah. I think you two have spoken already."

"Oh, yes indeed! So wonderful to meet the two of

you!" I say, greeting them with a wide smile.

"The pleasure is all mine. Any time I get an invite from Jack, I make sure to accept it. He's the sole reason I've reached where I am today; taught me everything I know," Ethan says.

Jack smiles and makes a dismissive gesture. "There wasn't much to teach, Ethan was always a natural in the kitchen."

"Don't I know it," Sarah quips. "He somehow manages to make something as seemingly simple as a hot chocolate into a life-changing experience."

Ethan and Sarah exchange one of those looks that could set the world on fire. Six months ago, that would have made me jealous, but now, it just makes me feel warm and fuzzy inside. I know what that feels like now, thanks to what Jack and I share.

"Ah, but the perfect hot chocolate recipe is far from easy to execute," I comment, which earns me Ethan's enthusiastic agreement.

"Exactly! There's a fine balance to it," he says.

Meanwhile, Amber appears behind me. She's been completely in her element organizing today's event, and creating buzz for it online. Her efforts have paid off, because despite the coffee shop now being double its original size, it's getting pretty busy already. Soon, we might need to start turning people away.

"You must be Sarah!" Amber reaches out to shake Sarah's hand. "I'm Amber. We've been emailing."

"Oh yes, so nice to finally meet in person," Sarah says. Almost instantly, they're absorbed in a conversation of their own.

I grin at both of them. "Excuse me for a moment, I'm going to go check on Deedee and the rest of the staff."

As I make my way towards the larger wood-framed glass case we've installed to show off our locally sourced artisanal baked goods, I sense Ethan and Jack hot on my heels.

"Something smells good," Ethan remarks. "Cinnamon rolls have always been my weakness… Oh, and you also have carrot cake?"

"Of course, and it's to die for," I say.

Ethan looks mesmerized by the display, which seems to amuse Jack, who is standing by with one of his crooked little smiles playing on his lips.

"Watch out, once you get hooked on these things, you'll find it impossible to control your waistline," Jack warns.

Ethan makes a dismissive gesture. "Ah, my waistline has always been a lost cause. Speaking of lost causes, is Callum coming?"

"Nah, he's busy conquering Scotland with his very own take on fish and seafood," Jack says. His words might not immediately express it, but I can hear the pride he feels for Callum's ongoing success. Both Ethan and him are the closest thing Jack has to best friends. Maybe that's what it's like when you spend long days in a commercial kitchen; you end up befriending those who work alongside or even underneath you.

"A cinnamon roll and a slice of carrot cake, then?" I ask, opening the sliding doors of the case.

"And of course a cappuccino to rescue me from the impending carb coma both of those treats will cause," Ethan adds with a wink.

"Good choice," I say, turning around to brew the drink myself, giving Deedee the chance to take a breather. The poor girl has been working her butt off the past few weeks, helping me pretty much with everything including getting the menus designed just right. How lucky that my formerly part time right hand woman has been learning graphic design on the side and was eager to prove her chops.

And even more lucky that Jack has finally managed to teach me the benefit of handing certain tasks off to trusted employees. Now that we've found each other, I certainly wouldn't want to end up married to the business, like he used to be.

I can barely hear the door chime over the buzz of excitement that has filled the room, as well as the hiss of the coffee machine, but manage to look up just in time to spot Sean and Lily walking in. I've met Jack's younger brother and his girlfriend a few times before, but every time I see them, I still can't get past how similar Sean and Jack are. They could be twins, if not for the fact that Jack's hair contains much more salt than pepper. Of course whenever I or Lily point that out, both of them furiously deny it, which is kind of cute.

"Lily, Sean, welcome!" I wave and call out to them. "Can I get you anything to drink while I'm at the machine already?"

Lily steps up first, leaning over the counter to squeeze my hand. "Wow, this place looks great, Alice! I'll have a mocha latte."

"Congrats, Alice," Sean says. "A double espresso for me, please."

"Thanks, you guys." I smile brightly at both of them. "I'm so glad you could make it, despite your busy shooting schedule."

"Of course, this is the perfect start to my awesome day off, as Lily likes to call them," Sean says, while shooting a knowing smile in his girl's direction. They're adorable together. Much like Jack, Sean has the absolute grumpiest TV persona, which perfectly fits the biting sense of humor he injects into his stand up comedy routines. But in person, he's just a great big softy.

"Sean." Jack gives his brother a slap on the back. "Good to see you."

"Likewise, big brother."

"No way, you guys are related?" Ethan asks, in

between bites of cinnamon roll. "I can't believe I never realized it!"

"What's this," Sean quips, "a Home TV networking event? And yeah, we are, strangely enough. But somehow Jack was born without a sense of humor."

"Alright, alright," Jack grumbles. "Meanwhile, I have seen you burn boiled eggs."

I suppress a grin. The two of them make a big display of teasing each other, especially in front of other people, but that's just how they express their affection. Luckily their intentions aren't lost on Ethan, who lets out a hearty laugh.

I turn around, pour the last drink, and arrange everything on a tray which I place on the counter in front of the four of them. "One cappuccino, a mocha latte, and a double shot of espresso."

"Thanks, Alice." Lily lifts her mug and raises it up before inhaling deeply. "I've been looking forward to this all morning."

"Cheers, Alice," Sean says.

Ethan meanwhile has polished off the entire cinnamon roll, which he washes down with a sip from his freshly brewed cappuccino. "Oh, Jack wasn't exaggerating when he said you make a terrific cup of coffee."

That little tidbit of information makes me grin all over again. High praise, especially coming from Jack, who isn't known for his compliments. I'm still floating, when a group of regulars makes a beeline for me. Of course they're here. My besties, my chosen family in a way, or at least they were long before I met Jack, opening up the possibility for a whole new kind of family…

They're a colorful bunch. Kayla, dressed in a glamorous knitted dress and knee high boots, Lauren, wearing one of her own designs—a lavender pant-suit and black silk blouse, Megan, whose darker complexion stands out beautifully against her powder blue tailored overcoat. And finally, Alexis, who is finally back in skinny jeans and a bright red leather jacket, after spending most of the end of the year in maternity wear. They try to swarm me, or at least, they would, if the counter wasn't in the way. I wipe my hands on my apron, and make my way around the till, and am immediately greeted with hugs and outpourings of praise and support.

"Wow, this place looks amazing!"

"Congratulations, Alice!"

"I can't believe what our regular old coffee hangout has turned into!"

"Awesome job, Alice!"

I don't even know who says what, and I try my best to thank all of them. But frankly, I'm overwhelmed in the best possible way.

"I couldn't have done it without you guys. I still

remember how hard it was at first when I started working here, and I didn't have a clue what I was doing. Still, you all would keep coming in every single week and support me," I tell them, suppressing a sniffle.

"Oh, now don't cry, Alice!" Kayla wraps her arm around me and pulls me against her. "We all feel the same way about you. No matter what was going on in all of our lives, we always had a home and a shoulder to lean on with you, at Coffee to the Rescue! And I for one am just so thrilled that it's going to stay here on the High Street forever."

I smile at her, then I smile at the rest of them. Now that everyone has grown busy in their own lives, we may not meet every single week anymore, but they're the best friends I could ask for.

"Girls!" Amber calls out, greeting them all with smiles and hugs. "Welcome!"

I'm still fighting off the growing lump in my throat when I remember all the events that led up to this moment.

I remember when Lauren first started coming in for takeaway coffees a little over a year ago. She was just in the process of opening her nearby boutique, when a weird mix-up with her coffee snagged her a date with one of London's most eligible bachelors. The rest, as they say, is history.

Kayla, who ended up falling for Lauren's dad of all

people! I remember consoling her after she found out, and feeling so relieved when I learned that it had all worked out a few weeks later.

Then, Megan, who didn't want to spend last Valentine's day alone, convinced me to try speed dating at the pub where Alexis works. The event itself was an abject failure for both of us, but she still ended up meeting the love of her life that night anyway.

And Alexis, the rough-around-the-edges bartender, who never seemed to have time for romance or fairy tales. Her stoic and sensible facade crumbled when she turned up for one of our weekly meet ups announcing an unplanned pregnancy. By her hot boss, no less! That was a shocker. And I'm so pleased they ended up talking things through and even tying the knot just when the baby arrived a couple of months ago.

Finally, Amber. Only six months ago, she was a basket case. So suspicious of men, bordering on paranoid. She'd perfect the art of keeping them at arm's length, while also relying on a series of them to subsidize her lifestyle, until it all went to hell and she ended up staying on my couch for a little while. She met Richard right here at the coffee shop, and everything changed for her. I barely even recognize her anymore, that's how much her outlook has changed ever since she started the PR agency that's been helping me grow my business.

They all mean so much to me, and so they are the ones I was looking forward to sharing today's launch with the most. And while I'm forced to leave them to their own conversations while making sure Deedee and the others continue to have everything under control, I do try to spend plenty of time with them. Who knows when we'll all get together like this again?

"Guys," Alexis speaks up after two rounds of coffee and baked treats. "I want to say something."

Immediately, everyone including myself grows quiet to listen to her.

"We've all had a busy year, and believe me, life with a newborn is definitely up there, but…" she turns to me to make sure I'm listening too. "Enough is enough. We can't keep on neglecting each other anymore. No more excuses. At least one Saturday a month, I want to see us all get together again."

A smile tickles the corner of my mouth. Because as busy as I've been preparing for today, and as blissful as the early days of my relationship with Jack have turned out to be, I've missed them all. Desperately. So, I can't think of a better way for today to end.

As the others start to agree one by one, my chest fills with emotion.

I've got it all now. All my dreams come true.

Not only do I have the business of my dreams as well as the man of my dreams, I'm about to have my friend group back as well. How could today possibly get any better?

***

It's early evening as the sun begins to set and the crowd of attendees thins. One by one, Ethan and Sarah, Sean and Lily, and every one of my friends say their goodbyes and leave. Finally, I take a moment to catch my breath, leaning against the counter and surveying the café. Today has turned out even better than I dared to hope for.

Jack comes up beside me, his hand resting gently on the small of my back. "You did it, Alice," he says softly.

I turn to face him, a smile spreading across my face. "I couldn't have done it without you," I say, my voice filled with emotion. "Thank you, Jack. For everything."

"Don't mention it." He leans in and kisses me, a soft, tender kiss that could bring tears to my eyes. "I love you, Alice."

"I love you too," I whisper back, my eyes meeting his.

We stand there, lost in each other's gaze, the world around us fading into the background. In this moment, it's just the two of us, and everything feels perfect. I could want for nothing.

"Alice," Jack says, his voice serious. "I want to ask

you something."

I look up at him. "Yes?"

He takes a deep breath, his eyes never leaving mine while he pauses. There's a sudden heaviness in the air between us which makes my heart pound. Because I can tell, this isn't a normal question. This isn't him wondering what I'd like for dinner, or where I've kept the keys to lock up. Still, I'm unprepared.

"Will you marry me?" His words shake me, unbalance me, and just about make me cry.

So much so, I'm unable to answer, at least at first. I'm just staring up at him with tears welling up in my eyes, unable to catch a breath.

And he looks helpless, bless him. Because he doesn't know. He doesn't know what I'm thinking, because I'm too clogged up with emotions to react properly.

"Yes," I say at last. My voice sounds forced, like a whimper or a squeak.

The relief that washes over his face is enough to allow me a full gasp of air.

"Yes, Jack, of course I'll marry you," I say. And as soon as I say that, I can't stop. Can't stop smiling. Can't stop staring at him. Can't stop the racing freight train rushing through my chest.

He smiles too, his eyes shining with unshed tears, and pulls me into a tight embrace. "I love you so much, Alice," he says, his voice filled with emotion.

"I love you too," I whisper back, feeling like the luckiest woman in the world.

As we stand there, wrapped in each other's arms, I know that now, this truly is it. Now I *really* have everything I could ever dream of. Until the next time he takes my breath away and surprises me with more. This is actually just the beginning of our journey together, the start of a new chapter. And I can't wait to see where it takes us, as long as it's together.

AUTHOR'S NOTE

Thanks so much for reading *Alice and the Grump!*

Perhaps you've been following me for a while, perhaps you're new to my work. But now that you're here, I'd like to give you a little background on how this book came to be...

My writing career started all the way back in October 2012 when I took a very deep breath, closed my eyes, crossed my fingers and even my toes and clicked 'Publish' on my first short story. That steamy little piece called *Ladies' Day*, and the book it grew into eventually (Beautiful Stranger) are still relevant today because it features a curvy heroine and her more mature lover. It serves as my first foray into steamy body positive romance.

Since then, I've published a whole bunch of books, in various romance sub genres; as L. Moone I write contemporary, and as Lorelei Moone I write about shifters, vampires and other paranormals. Certain themes tend to repeat themselves throughout my catalogue.

Beauty lies in the eye of the beholder. The hang-ups we tend to have about ourselves and our bodies often aren't shared by the opposite sex. While it's a lot more popular to write about gorgeous curvy ladies and their athletic admirers than the other way around, I've dabbled in both in the past. I just never felt there was a big market for husky men in romance (my sales numbers supported this notion, unfortunately). 2020 changed that thanks to Jessa Kane and her sexy big boy titles, *Hefty* and *Husky*. My mind was blown, and I absolutely devoured them and couldn't get enough. I'm slowly seeing other authors enter this space, so perhaps the time has come? I hope so, because I'd love to write (and read!) a whole bunch more of these...

Alice has been around for years, ever since I started writing Coffee & Curves in 2019. And after spending so much time with her in that series, it was only obvious that sooner or later she would get a book of her own. Funnily enough, Jack is even older than that, in the sense that he's been around since appearing in a side role in my first ever book about a celebrity chef, Only a Taste, from around a decade ago. Beyond that, he's also been mentioned in my Husky Men Do It Better series, as Ethan's mentor in Recipe for Passion, and his restaurant serves as the location where Sealed with a Kiss is shot.

Finally, these two lonely souls are no longer alone, and Alice has finally been able to achieve her professional dream too. From lowly employee, she's now the proud owner of Coffee to the Rescue, which will surely remain a favorite setting for future books of mine set in the fictionalized London suburb of Teddington...

What's next for me? Let's see... A whole lot more curvy girl/dad bod books, that's for sure. Once you've worked your way through my backlist, below, do consider signing up for my newsletter (I'll give you a free book if you do!), and you'll be among the first to know when a knew title drops. :-)

Please scroll down for all the links to my other books and series.

And that's enough from me. I hope you enjoyed the story as much as I did while writing it.

x, Lorelei